The Boss Dog

A STORY BY

M. F. K. FISHER

The Boss Dog

PANTHEON BOOKS
New York & San Francisco

Library of Congress Cataloging-in-Publication Data

Fisher, M.F.K. (Mary Frances Kennedy), 1908-
The Boss Dog : a story of Provence / M.F.K. Fisher.
         p.   cm.
         ISBN 0-679-73860-6 (pbk.)
         1. Dogs—Fiction.   I. Title.
         PS3511.I7428B6   1992
         813'.54—dc20   91-53117

Manufactured in the United States of America
4689753

Contents

The Boss Dog

The Boss Dog

Most people who wander together have good things happen to them, and possibly the best thing that happened to Anne and Mary and their mother as they wandered from California to Aix-en-Provence, a serene old town near Marseille in France, was to meet the Boss Dog very soon after they arrived.

If they had not met him, and had not been selected, or so it seemed to them, to absorb some of his sinister yet beneficent spell, their lives might have been quite different.

Once, he even rescued one of them. And once he taught them about not judging too hastily as to whether a man who looks like a thug-mug-crook is that or something else again. Several times he taught them little tricks of bravery or bravado, or how to cock an ear at Fate, or how, when all is said and done, to survive, in one form or another. (In his own case, he did the last the surest way, like most of the rest of us!)

But the day the two little American girls and their mother

met this gay rascal, they had no idea of what his influence would be on them. . . .

It was late in September when they first went into the Café Glacier on the big square or at least five-sided circle (a square circle or even a circle with sides is an impossibility, of course, except in Aix-en-Provence . . .), and they sat down at one of the tables just inside the windows of the restaurant.

They felt tired and a little depressed, for the town was not their own town, everybody spoke French instead of American, and an endless procession of electric- and gas-driven buses and explosive little scooters called Vespas roared around the five-sided square or square circle.

In the middle of it was the enormous and monumental and very tall fountain called *La Grande Fontaine* or *La Fontaine de la Rotonde* or simply The Big One. It was built in layers of lions-dolphins-turtles-swans-cherubs, and finally some bearded heads of men, and on top three large well-endowed women. All, except the last, spat, spurted, splashed, spluttered, and spouted in every direction.

The three smaller flesh-and-blood women felt confused.

Anne took off her gloves. She put them into the pocket of her coat, and then got them out again and began to bite gently at the tip of the third finger of the left one, which was of white cotton and quite dirty and her favorite, because of a lingering agreeable taste of vanilla that never seemed to wash away.

Mary put her gloves in her pocket, her elbows on the table, and her chin in her hands. She might be dozing off. . . .

The mother of the girls, one of whom was eleven and one

going on nine, took off her gloves and put them in her pocket, put her chin in her hands and one finger almost in her mouth, and then said, "Anne, please take your glove out of your mouth. Mary, please take your elbows off the table. I'm tired. I'm dead. What would you like to drink?"

A waiter was, as if by magic (the kind that good waiters learn early if not at birth and most people never appreciate), standing by their table. He quirked his eyes and at the same time his ears at them, the way good and even bad waiters do, and you could see his mind writing on a little piece of paper, invisible in his hand. Tired woman, it wrote. Two tired nice-looking little girls. Tourists and may be in a hurry. Probably want ice cream. . . .

"Well, what do you want, or do you?" the mother asked in a polite cranky voice.

She felt so weary and so inexplicably far away from home that what she really wanted to do was lie down in the middle of the five-sided square circle, except that the Big Fountain was already there with three marble women on it, and go boo-hoohoo . . . more waterworks. So instead she allowed herself to snap gently at the two people she loved most in the world, which is an odd but not unusual kind of behavior.

Mary looked vaguely through the wall of the restaurant, which was of glass and therefore very easy to look through, and without seeing anything she was looking at, because she was too tired, she said, "Oh, it doesn't matter. Maybe some vodka."

Mary always said this when she was exhausted, and it was a

signal to her mother that she was at the far limits of her energy, and that she was remembering one time when she was barely old enough to walk, when she had by accident drunk a sip of vodka and gone roaring and rolling and spewing across the floor like a little wild bear.

Now the mother peered at her, and seeing that her eyes were still turned in a dreamy unfocused way on the Big Fountain, looked up once more at the waiter, standing doing what he was supposed to do, which was wait.

"Anne?" she asked somewhat more patiently, for already in this quiet glassy room she felt less tired, less alone.

Anne took the end of the vanilla-finger of the left glove out of her mouth, for suddenly it tasted really revolting. "Me? Who? Me? What?"

A few more buses gunned by. Little Vespa scooters scooted by. A man with a Siamese cat perched tiltingly on one shoulder limped by, and then a pretty lady with tiny feet in high heels and tiny twin boys in a double pram teetered by. Everybody seemed to be going someplace and happy and busy except the mother and her girls, and they were really worn out and, if three people can be lonely together, they were.

The waiter was still standing there, though, and the mother looked at Anne again and said, "Well, do say what you want. *Decide*." Then she said, "Please, darling honey-bun and sweet potato," for that was her way of admitting that she was sorry to be cross.

Anne said very nicely, "I would like some ice cream. I

would like some vanilla ice cream and if there is by accident no vanilla I would like some strawberry."

She looked firmly at her mother.

The waiter, who understood a little English or at least American, glanced rather like a rabbit who can choose between a carrot and a leaf of lettuce between Anne and her mother, and then said in French, "Today there happens to be no vanilla and also by chance no strawberry because summer is almost a thing of the past, BUT today there happens to be chocolate, and it is very good but VERY good.

"I believe," he added, as firmly as if he clasped his invisible pad of paper in one hand like a little prayer book and was already writing something upon it, "that One, a Certain Young Lady, will like or even love the chocolate."

The mother savored the subtleties and the comprehension of this announcement, in a language still too subtle and all-comprehensive for her children.

Mary looked quietly around the room, empty now at a too-early "tea-time," for the traveling Englishmen who normally drank tea were at a horseshow or snoozing or sketching the countryside, and the people who lived in Aix seldom drank tea in public.

Anne, who would have liked to speak directly to the waiter and get things underway, in no matter what limping French, looked politely at her mother as she had accustomed herself to do if she wished easy sailing; her mother, who in turn would have been delighted to see somebody else take control of things but had been taught that children should let their elders talk to waiters, in no matter what language, said, "Two chocolate ice creams, please, and a small coffee. And a large brandy."

"*D'accord, Madame*," the waiter said, which was a rather lazy slangy way of agreeing with a customer but which he did not mean at all impertinently: he felt that these three people would turn out to be his friends, and it did turn out that they would be and were. He swerved off, flushing slightly.

Whoever was in the kitchen at this odd hour of about 4:12 in the afternoon put a generous unordered dollop of whipped cream under and around the chocolate ice cream for each girl, and they licked at it as if they wished they were little kittens and not two children who had to sit up fairly straight in an empty French restaurant with people going past the windows all the time. If they had been able to grow long tails right then, they would have curled them happily around their haunches or flanks or bottoms and then later licked them in long strokes, remembering that cream.

After eating most of what the waiter had brought them, except the dishes and silverware, which in Aix is rather complicated because an ice cream is served in a stemmed metal cup on a plate and then there is a glass of cold water in which stands the spoon, cooling, to eat the ice with, with a thin brown cookie called a *gaufrette* stuck up like a signal; after attending to all this caloric panoply, Anne and Mary leaned back, feeling much better.

Their mother leaned back too; the world outside the glass wall was not as loud and dusty to her.

Anne removed a small dab of cream from one side of her mouth, which otherwise was as impeccable as that of an ivory statue.

"That is a very interesting dog who is going to come in," she said.

"What do you mean, 'That is a very interesting dog who is going to come in'?" Mary asked. "Probably what you mean is, if you really mean it, is that what you mean is, 'Look at that dog who may come in.' He may be interesting to you, but how can you state that he is also interesting to us? And how do you——?"

"What dog?" The mother asked such a question in an apologetic way that by now was quite automatic. She was always asking things like that in that way, because she was always or quite often off dreaming about this or that while the girls were talking about other thises and thats which seemed to be fairly unrelated to her own.

"Oh, for heaven's sake! Oh, murder!" they both said in a kind and patient way, for by now the cream and stuff in their stomachs was making them so, much more efficaciously than if they had drunk only the water with the spoons in it. "Look. There he is. There he goes."

They all looked toward the door onto the great square circle, where the buses went whirling by and where the fountain splashed and spat, and where there seemed to be a gentle endless tide of old and middle-aged and young women and baby carriages, all full of children either about to be born or eight months old, the latter smiling and cackling and waving.

The door closed. Some of the outside noises stopped. The waiter, who later came to be known as Léon, except on Wednesdays when Paul took over for him, opened the door and then closed it again, as if to assure himself that a human had done it and not a four-footed fellow, and Boss Dog walked slowly across the room toward Anne and Mary.

He was the doggiest dog anyone ever saw, just the way you can say that a Mexican-Yankee-Frenchman-Greek is the most Mexican-Yankee-French-Greek individual you ever saw, summing up all of himself as such, up to his cocky wonderful ears in whatever he is doing. This fellow was everything a creature could possibly be of HIM, of HE. He was Boss Dog.

Anne recognized him at once as something ultimate.

"Look at him," she said in a voice which a few years later she might well use for a person as yet unmet called a Majarajah. She spoke firmly and posedly, leaning on every syllable.

Mary was looking. Her large prune-brown eyes first grew larger and then narrowed with a kind of secondary recognition, as if she had just seen somebody like King Arthur, unexpectedly, and after a quick halt had said hurriedly, "Oh, yes! That's King Arthur!"

"Wow," she said.

The mother agreed, without a word.

The dog, who had come off the *Place de la Grande Fontaine*,

10

took a quick sharp glance around, and then trotted toward the back of the restaurant: the dim bar, the toilets and cloak-rooms, the pantries, the fine smelly kitchens. He plainly had his rounds to make, and he showed it in the stance of his black tail, which turned up arrogantly over the short white hairs of his behind.

He was a large fellow with a fat rear, mostly the kind of terrier called yippy, part Fox and part Boston and part Mystery, a rather rat-nosed, narrow-eyed, undistinguished dog esthetically, except for his unusually long plump full beautiful ear, and its peculiar mate.

The coal black one fell down soft and helpless and lovable over his left eye. The other, white and crisp as celery, stood up so proudly that it seemed to draw his right eye with it, into a merry shrewd questioning look. It was as if Boss Dog wore a hat which had been born onto him when he himself was born, pulling his face into a mask of meek velvety guile on one side and of cocky-mockery on the other.

He seemed to know it, this contradiction. As he went to the kitchens he turned fleetingly toward the table where Anne and Mary sat with their mother, and his soft black left ear had probably never looked so soft, and his stiff white ear standing out from his bold head had never looked so mocking. He knew his own dramatic allure, it was clear.

He disappeared, busily.

"There's a dog for you," Anne said. " 'Wow' is right."

"He is plainly," Mary said, coming to life as if she had always been so instead of lately half-dead, "plainly and indefinitely the boss of this whole place. Indefinitely, he is KNOWN here."

"He's the kind of dog adventures would happen around," Anne said wistfully, hopefully. "Gangsters. Or witches. You can tell that he would be able to handle them."

"I think we should come back here tomorrow," Mary said as they got into gloves and so forth, and in a vague but active way the mother felt that instead of being tourists drifting about, they had suddenly GOT someplace, that they were indeed THERE, besides just staying in a decorous boarding-house.

Something about the way the dog had trotted efficiently in from the square circle, the way the waiter had politely opened the door and closed the door for him after he himself had done so, as if to prove that it was perfectly normal, made her feel settled and even established, and she smiled companionably at the three monumental females on top of the great busy spouting fountain.

"I think we should too," she said. "We'd better ask what the waiter's name is."

The Time He
Sat Down Twice

In a surprisingly short time after Anne and Mary felt that they were *there* in Aix instead of perching, which is the usual state of wanderers in any country at all, even their own, they found themselves trotting around town just about the way Boss Dog did, knowing exactly where they were going and what for and why. And since like everybody else he walked up and down the Cours Mirabeau several times a day, that is where they usually saw him, being there too.

The Cours Mirabeau is probably the most beautiful Main Street in the world. A great many people have said so, in prose and verse and even poetry, for hundreds of years, and have seldom been contradicted, except perhaps on the dueling field.

Guidebooks, which always have a lot of other things to mention, usually do their best lightly by describing it as "wide and shaded, with many fountains, some dating to 36 B.C.," or something like that, which is true, of course, but inadequate.

It has several fountains of different periods of design, going down the middle. One, maybe the best, is called Old Mossback and is a great ugly lump of furry stone dribbling fairly smelly water, warm enough to send up steam on cold days, in which old aching people dip their wrists and dabble at their eyes. The others are more elegant, people and fountains both.

And the Cours is without a doubt one of the widest as well as shadiest streets that anyone has ever dreamed of: four majestic rows of giant plantain trees, with their roots down in a hidden river, rising up a hundred feet or more, straight and beautiful, and then meeting, artfully trimmed for it in the springtime, to form a thick green shade in summer, a delicate lacy cage in winter, a long three-arched tunnel from one end of the Cours at the *Place de la Grande Fontaine* for about a half-mile to the other, where a noble statue of King René stands, with him holding a bunch of grapes and smiling proudly enough at all this fine balance of the town he helped give it to.

He looks down the row of living fountains between him and The Big One. He seems to be listening to their ceaseless music. Now and then a little truck or even a Vespa bumps into one of their sides, and the police come and turn off the splashing for a few minutes, but in general the Old King sees to it that the whole Cours spouts and murmurs properly, and that it ripples with green shade when the time is right. . . .

In the summer the shade on that long street is so deep that people walking in it feel like fish in the bottom of a deep clean river. The great plantains are like immeasurably tall reeds. The air is pure and sweet and sifted, somewhat as river water should be to an unbothered fish. There is room to exist.

Even the sidewalks are as wide as most streets, with stone benches along them where old women knit and talk and jiggle their baby buggies now and then, and room for everybody in Aix to stroll and meet and stroll on again, room for perhaps hundreds of bright chairs around dozens of little round tables in the green dimness of summer shade or the thinner golden light of winter through the bare branches, or the tremulous green-gold of spring.

There are ten or so cafés behind the little tables, most of them pleasant both inside and out under the tall trees, but the ones preferred by Anne and Mary and by Boss Dog, who was something of an instinctive snob or at least somewhat as persnickety as they, were his own Glacier at one end of the Cours, owned by the dog and his stylishly dressed mistress, and the Deux Garçons at the other end, near the statue of the quiet smiling king.

The Glacier was considered a social upstart, having been there only about two hundred and thirty-four years in various guises. The Deux Garçons still kept its blotched mirrors and bespeckled candelabra, and had for a few more centuries or at least generations been a private chess club for the gentle-men of the Cours and a restricted number of affluent trades-people.

One of these upper-class pubs had a star for gastronomy in the current *Guide Michelin*, and one wasn't even mentioned, and each felt dashingly proud and set up about its own form of ignominy, and went right on serving its own version of what people would like to eat and drink.

The girls and their mother soon got into the agreeable Aix-ois habit of stopping at either the one or the other for lem-onade hot chocolate vanilla ice cream dry vermouth brandy even coffee even plain soda water, on an average of several times a week if not daily and, just as soon, they noticed that while Boss Dog paid only a curt disapproving attention to the people in the numerous cafés along the Cours, he always made a leisurely tour of the tables at the Deux Garçons, to check on how many of his own clients were spending their money with his friendly rival.

He never wasted any time on the soft looks and bribes and seductive finger-snappings of the average "dog lover," but it was plain that he recognized the three Americans, and that he forgave them for straying occasionally from the Glacier, as long as they went on up to the Deux Garçons: he would slow down his quick efficient inspection long enough to sniff at them, give them a sharp look, and then trot away.

Once, the first or second day of school, he stopped short at their table, obviously pretending to be indifferent to them.

Anne, who knows immediately what is on a dog's mind,

held down her new reading book for him to smell, which he did, in a casual way.

"He probably thinks a second-grade reader is baby stuff," Mary said with some embarrassment. "Which it is."

"Well, you'll be put up a few grades as soon as you learn enough French," her mother said for perhaps the tenth time that day, because both girls were tremulous inside, new in school, looming above the sharp dark little children of Provence like great thick white moths, and bumbling and fumbling with their words. "Anyway," she went on in spite of her pain for them, "all that matters to the Boss Dog, I imagine, is whether you are enrolled in Sainte Catherine or La Nativité. He's a real snob. I've heard that this year La Nativité is more stylish. He may disapprove of you two girls, stuck with the Dominicans."

"But they are very broadminded," Anne gently reminded her mother of what she herself had been reminded several times lately. "Very tolerant. And very patient with foreigners."

The Boss Dog sniffed again at her book, made a short sound which could have been the beginning of a cough or the end of a sneeze, and hurried off.

"He obviously prefers Sainte Catherine. You can tell he approves," Mary said somewhat dryly, "by his tail." Then she added, "Thank goodness."

"Yes," Anne said. "There's something about the way he trots away. The tail. You can tell everything is all right. I'd hate to have him against me."

"Maybe we'd better have lunch at the Glacier on Sunday, instead of just tea," the mother said. "Stay on his good side."

She thought she was being a little funny, but it was not that way, really. That Sunday noon was the first time they ever saw the Boss Dog sit down.

It had been a very busy day for him, with every table of the Glacier filled, both inside and outdoors under the bright umbrellas and the rustling falling leaves, and extra buses loaded with holiday trippers to be met and inspected on several of the five sides of the round square, and an unusual number of other dogs to be kept in order.

Boss was breathing fast and was plainly growing a little irritable by the time Anne and Mary had finished lunch and then three "late" peaches each, four bananas between them, and two large bunches of grapes for dessert. So far he had not raised his voice, but had managed by merely walking fast, and frowning, to scare off four poodles and a boxer who would have liked to sniff around for some crumbs or even a chicken bone under the *terrasse* tables.

The dogs on leashes were not much bother, but in the warm late-autumn air a great many masters, out for a digestive or perhaps merely meditative stroll after church-and-dinner (with the traditional Sunday treat of little cakes from the pastry shop at the corner), had loosened not only their belts but their discipline, and as everybody knows, lower-class animals if given an inch will take a mile.

Thoroughbreds never made much real trouble for the Boss. It was the dogs more or less like himself, offspring of the people, poor misbegotten devils he understood and loved and hated as he did his own sons, who made his hackles rise, and Sundays were the toughest days for him.

On this one, he coped nippily with the post-Mass crowds, and the normal strollers on such a fine holiday, and exerted all of his large fund of self-control with the mixture of high and low castes during the leisurely mealtime. But when at about two-thirty he discovered that a skinny and completely undistinguished terrier-type had slipped in past his patrol and was begging at a table over toward the trolley-bus station on the terrace, he could no longer hold back his fatigue and exasperation, and he let out a clear-cut snarl.

"Watch it! Watch it, fellow," Mary muttered toward him.

Anne turned around in her chair, just in time to see him lunge with unexpected clumsiness straight between the waiter Léon's legs.

There was, as inevitably as yes with no or pepper with salt, a crash that was all the more deafening because the tray which had spun from Léon's hands and landed on the sidewalk was empty. There is nothing as noisy as an empty metal tray crashing to the pavement, as is well known.

It was the fact of this emptiness and the tray's resultant ability to spring about and roll and clatter, that caused so many other things to fall, crash and make a general mess, in the midst of which the skinny fox-terrier made off forever with a piece of bread in his mouth and his ignoble tail tucked under his rump.

Léon (a conglomerate title of trust by then), trying to catch the spinning tray and at the same time deafen his ears to the sound he had perhaps heard before from it, lunged against a small serving table on which Angelo, the head waiter, was heating a service of *bourride* for four latecomers dressed somewhat surprisingly but nattily in riding habits.

(*Bourride* is a fish soup made in Provence that should be made oftener and in more places, and it involves a chafing dish over an alcohol lamp, several bowls for the soup, whole small fishes and sliced bigger ones that have been cooked to make the soup, fresh slices of bread, and a kind of thick sauce called *aioli* to stir in at the last, with fresh lemons from another plate . . . really an amusing and pleasant way to eat a boiled fish, and as complicated as the cook wants to make it, involving countless accoutrements.)

Poor Léon, seeing that he was destined to crash within seconds into the whole setup for the *bourride*, tried hard to shift his energies from catching his galloping tray to catching the alcohol lamp in his path . . . and by sending everything else that was on the serving table into several laps, he managed to do so, and stood panting, rather like a male Statue of Liberty, with his flame held flickering but aloft over a fairly messy scene. Rich creamy soup, odorous with all the herbs of Provence, ran down the riding-trousers of two of the four hungry diners. At the table next to them a fat man wore, like an orchid on his shoulder, a seven-inch wolf-fish which the cook had artfully managed to cook whole, even to its angry eyes and insolent curved tail.

Next to the man a fat woman, who was fairly probably his

wife, because they looked as alike as married people are supposed to, wore the wolf-fish's wife or girlfriend, not on her
shoulder but partly down the little canyon of her bosom, and
man woman and two fish they all had their mouths open wide
in the same astonishment.

All around, there were crisp slices of bread and wedges of
lemon on the pavement, and the air smelled deliciously of
spilt *bourride* in general and the ferocious garlic of a spilt *bourride* with *aioli* in particular.

Anne and Mary reached into the basket on their table for
more grapes, their eyes pained, in an unconscious attempt to
make things look normal.

Léon started the deft and apologetic mopping-up which
any good waiter has at his fingertips, helped by the equally
deft and apologetic Angelo, and a crew of small pale kitchen
apprentices, and the stylish owner relayed a hurry-call to the
cook for more and even better *bourride*, and it was discovered
that almost everything but the fat woman's bosom had been
tailored of moisture-proof material and was therefore easily
dabbed clean.

People sat back, drank an extra sip of pink wine, and smiled
again.

It was then that Mary, who was extremely watchful of such
things and had been keeping an eye on the reactions of the
Boss Dog, saw that he was sitting down.

"Hey," she murmured urgently to Anne and her mother.
"Hey. Look. Quick."

They did, and felt a mutual amazement to see the dapper

fellow actually relaxed this far. He had a surprisingly large if well-designed bottom, and his tail went out in a perfect example of practical logistics and balance along the sidewalk in back, like a kangaroo's or perhaps better like an angle-iron, so that all of a sudden he gave the impression of having been made in order to *sit*, like a Buddha. His back legs stuck forward frankly and flatly but without looking ridiculous, and so unexpectedly large was his rear that his front legs seemed hardly necessary for his general balance, again like a Buddha.

His tongue hung out discreetly for air, and on his proud face under the black ear and the white there was a look of great fatigue.

Anne was full of pity. "He's embarrassed," she said softly, suffering for anyone else so proud and sensitive. "He only did his duty."

"What a crash, what a juicy crash," Mary said. "But it could have been even worse. I don't know how, but it could have. If Léon had been *carrying* the soup, for instance. . . ." She looked happy, listening with her third ear to the resonant liquid explosion that would have resulted. . . .

"It was bad enough," Anne said. "And all because of that horrible ugly unattractive sneaky little dog that crept in."

"He couldn't help being horrible, probably," the mother said, automatically seizing the chance to utter a little moral dictum.

"Born horrible, die horrible," Mary said coldly.

"Not at all," the mother said hurriedly if blindly. "But he was obviously hungry and he took his chance, very bravely, too, to get in behind the Boss's back. He was only obeying his instincts." She felt rather silly, as usual in such a situation.

"Then he wasn't being brave. You don't have to be brave to obey your instincts. You just have to be dumb and *do* it. Obey, I mean," Mary explained.

The mother felt like saying, Oh, hell, but she was trying to remember that Mary was going on nine and hated loose or profane talk. "Well, I agree with Anne," she said, pretending not to retreat. "It must be rather embarrassing for the Boss to have started such an upheaval."

Anne hissed a quick SSSHHHH at her, but it was too late: the dog had heard.

He got up slowly from his godlike squat, reestablished his balance upon his four legs, and looked squarely at the mother for an infinitely painful second.

Then he turned away, past the kitchen boys sweeping and mopping discreetly at the scene of the late disaster, past the leathery legs of the four people in riding habits and the plump silky feet of the two Fat Ones next to them and formerly in the direct path of the downpour, past the silver champagne buckets which Angelo had placed with consummate tact beside the riders and Fat Ones, to make them forget the spots on their trousers and the sliding fish in even more intimate places. . . .

The Boss Dog walked toward the door into the darkest regions of the restaurant, gave one last sharp look toward the bus stations, and disappeared.

Anne sighed heavily. "Excuse me for deeming to criticize

you," she said with dripping sarcasm to her mother, "but you shouldn't have said that so loudly. He's very sensitive. He may even leave for Marseille."

Oh, rubbish, the mother felt like saying, so said it inaudibly. A fine thing if I can't even speak American in front of a French dog. She decided to have a brandy.

"He heard you, all right," Mary said.

Across the circle of street that went around the huge fountain in the middle of the five-sided square or whatever it was that was called *La Rotonde* the sound of the numberless spoutings and splashings came to them in a traffic lull. Love that fountain, the mother thought. It's the busiest noisiest anywhere, with babies turtles porpoises lions birds men all spitting like mad, splash splash, layers and layers of brimming widening basins playing one into another, pigeons flying through the spray, light shining on and through, really the way a fountain should want to be, if I were a fountain for instance, so lively and silly and encouraging. . . .

"Wake up. I still say, for the third time, that he was only doing his duty," Anne said, looking down at her cluttered fruit plate with a remote pale expression which on anyone else, except perhaps Eleanora Duse or Anna Magnani, would be hammy.

"Oh, for Pete's sake," the mother said, watching her language.

"Well," Mary said defensively, for rather like a saint of other days she was scared to go out to the long hall to the bathroom alone but would defend her sister without thought

24

or fear against a thousand stinking devils, "I agree with Anne. He was only doing his duty. His mistress should be *proud*, proud *indeed*, that he protected the restaurant from outside dogs and especially sneaky little ones that try to steal and cadge and welch and whatever. Léon . . . *Léon* should be proud to have him around to help. Well, it was a mess for a few minutes but not the Boss's fault. Léon should be proud to have him here!"

"And I should be proud to have a poached fish hop down my bosom," the mother said, and they all laughed and went up the Cours Mirabeau, where that day the fountains in the middle of the waxy gleaming street seemed to spout with a special enthusiasm.

The wide sidewalks on both sides of the dim green tunnel, all the cafés and bookstores on one side and the candy shops and tearooms and art galleries on the other, were crowded with people moving like fish, tranquilly, below the shade in the shifting light. Girls pushed against boys, and older lovers against their loves, and always the ancient women knitted on the stone benches and joggled the baby carriages now and then over their timeless mumblings one to another. All the little tables were covered with glasses of lemonade-chocolate-beer-vermouth-brandy and with silver cups stained with the dregs of ice cream. Waiters skimmed here and there, and the leaves drifted down.

Anne and Mary went out into the middle of the Cours, looking to right and left for traffic, and dabbled their hands at Old Mossy Back, where warm water from the same springs as the old Roman baths of Aix spouted out over its thick green-black coat. It was a kind of ritual with them, none could tell why. The day was so balmy that no steam rose from the basin, and because it was Sunday nobody stood there to fill a pitcher or to bathe old aching wrists and eyes. . . .

Then later at the Deux Garçons, where they drank hot chocolate because it was six o'clock and growing chilly, the Boss Dog dropped in for a minute.

After a quick once-over of the general tone of the clientele, which was of course somewhat low on Sundays but picked up when the weekend riffraff cleared out for supper, he glanced toward the table where the three Americans sat trying not to watch him.

They tried not to breathe even, waiting for what he would do next, for they, as perhaps nobody else there, knew what his day had been, in professional hazard and humiliation.

He turned his head so that his soft black ear fell down over his eye and so that his crisp white ear was away from them, and thus they could not read what he was saying. And then, to their astonishment, he sat down.

That is, they were astonished because he sat down *again*, for the second time that day, and because he sat down beside *them*.

It was only for a few seconds. They all looked at one another. He seemed to move his ears a little up and down. He sighed gently. Almost immediately he gathered his rather ridiculously big fat rump up under him again, reestablished his balance from Buddhistic to canine, and hurried off as if it had never been he at all. . . .

"Wow," Mary said. "He looked bushed."

"No, but a little desperate," Anne explained. "He is exhausted, right enough. That awful scene this morning when he rescued Léon. . . . "

"*He* rescued *Léon*!? Hah!"

"Well, he did his duty," Anne repeated with protective dignity. "That awful *bourride* everywhere! And I feel that he has forgiven you, I mean us, for mentioning it in front of him," she said, glancing in a kindly way at her mother.

"Yes, it seemed to me he smiled, just faintly of course," Mary said in a noncommittal way.

"Well, thank God," the mother said. "Does either of you want some more hot chocolate?"

The Time He Coped with the Mob

Anne and Mary thought that once the Boss Dog had admitted them enough to his intimacy to sit down twice in front of them, and once actually *beside* them, he would continue this open friendly behavior. They were mistaken. They did not know dogs of his haughty and suspicious nature. He resumed his old closed pattern of conducting himself, and as of the next day, Monday, met them face to face on the Cours Mirabeau without a glance.

"You'd think he'd never seen us before," Anne said despondently, as if she were saying (which in a way she was), ". . . after all we've suffered and gone through for him," for she had indeed endured tortures the day before, with the *bour-ride* all over things and people at the Glacier and the Boss having to be humble about causing it. "You'd think he didn't even like us."

"Maybe he doesn't," Mary said. "Who do we think we are, anyway?"

"Well," the mother said, "who do we? Or is it whom? I mean, think we are? Who are we?"

She felt rather mean to put it that way, but it might change the subject, and she sensed that Anne could easily slide into nether dumps about the foolish fat-rumped café hound. It might be sagacious to encourage her to feel morbid about her own *two*-leggedness and her own self. . . .

The conversation about The Origin of Man, or Woman, lasted until they got to the Kursaal on the five-sided Rotonde, one of the shabbier and more stylish movie theaters in Aix, where they were going to a matinee with Fernandel in it: the mother had discovered that even when Fernandel played tragic small-town doctors in love with tarts the children found him basically funny and therefore satisfying.

It is only for so-called adults that tragedy becomes important, she told herself somewhat pompously . . . children know all the time that people like Chaplin and Fernandel are just as sad as they are themselves, and therefore they don't worry about it.

The movie was, in fact, supposed to be a comedy, which with the current General Run of French movies, which this was, meant that it was carelessly directed and composed, so that moments of almost painfully amusing and brilliant comedy alternated with equally painful drivel, cinematographically and every other way. It did not matter to Anne and Mary, as long as Fernandel's beautiful monkey-face was there.

"I feel as if he were me or I were he or him or however," Anne said once, trying to look like him and succeeding, in spite of their different bones, sexes, and ages.

The film was supposed to be a spoofing of American Westerns and gangster pictures, and every now and then it was wonderful, like Anne trying to *feel* like Fernandel and now and then at least *looking* like him.

It started and ended with cowboys riding into a deliberately cardboard sunset, clippityclop, and in between there were a couple of fine things about racketeers and their molls and the Third Degree. Lights burned down on Fernandel and his poker-faced inquisitors, who kept puffing cigaret smoke at him until they were all blind and coughing and only he was fresh, clear-eyed, and of course innocent. The closeups were meant to be horrible: slit-eyes, slit-mouths, and clenched mean jaws moving fiendishly up and down on their chewing gum. . . .

Mary leaned across Anne to her mother and spoke thickly through a mouthful of half-melted chocolate, which they had bought from the nice woman who went up and down the aisles selling it from a little tray that seemed to grow out from her stomach.

"What did she say?" the mother hissed at Anne, over the whuffing cruel sounds of the detectives blowing smoke at Fernandel. She blinked helplessly at her daughters, her eyes almost blinded. She felt like going into a long voluptuous fit of coughing, along with the animal-faced detectives. Anne sighed resignedly.

Mary leaned once more toward her mother over her sister, and blew moist chocolate air and a few stifled syllables at them, for she, too, hated to disturb the general feeling of hypnotized acceptance that should and usually does reign during any movie at all, from Mickey Mouse to The Robe of Christ.

Anne sighed again, super-patiently and patently, and whispered, "She says the Boss Dog ought to be here."

"Oh."

The mother leaned back and managed to focus her eyes once more on the Third Degree, with Fernandel looking healthier and more simian all the time and the lights showing up more and more sinister scars and disease-pits on his lean interrogators.

Then she whispered, "Why?"

Anne sighed one more time, but was brave and honorable about it and replied dutifully, in a gust only slightly less rich and moist than Mary's, "Because he would know how to *handle* gangsters."

"Oh."

It was of course simple, thus explained. The Boss Dog did indeed have something about him, a kind of cool arrogance, which smacked of every tense hard-drinking ascetically debauched detective spawned in city slums to track down his brothers on the opposite side of Right, Justice, and The Law. The way he walked across the sidewalk and looked once and once only at a bus full of Sunday trippers or overfed habitués of his restaurant; the way he had but to make one sharp move toward a possible or actual interloper; the way he could droop his soft velvety black ear when he needed, as all tough heroes do, a moment of tenderness: all this was plainly part of a fast-moving story of murder-larceny-rape-THE MOB, and as the mother led Anne and Mary out into the dusky *Place de la Rotonde* and toward the Glacier, it seemed quite natural to have one of them say, "There he goes."

It was the Boss all right, walking quickly and nippily past them and around the big fountain. A bus for Marseille swerved just enough to miss him, and an old man heading his horsecart homeward from a day at the Grain Market pulled hard on his reins, to let the dog progress without even a swish of his tail toward the lighted restaurant.

"It was good," Mary said. "I bet he enjoyed it . . . all those blinding lights in the Third Degree . . . Fernandel did, I mean, and also Boss."

"I need a ham sandwich desperately," Anne said in a quiet way.

"I thought it was good too," the mother said. "But I honestly think it is slightly exaggerated, if not deliberately zany, to pretend that damn fool dog was there, too, sitting in a seat at a hundred and fifty francs a whack and enjoying Fernandel."

"You're tired," Mary said. "Anyway, he was there. And maybe he gets in cheaper on a student's card." She cackled.

"And a large glass of milk," Anne said.

33

As is often the case, some good food judiciously chosen and then eaten made many things look brighter, if no less ridiculous, and the girls and their mother felt fine, leaning over a few crumbs, some empty glasses, and their plates stripped of everything but two inches of ham rind on one of them, and a smear of mustard.

They talked amiably of what little stinkers some of the schoolchildren were and what glamor-girls some others, and of what a shame it was that Cézanne's old studio had none of the old man's sketches or even doodlings in it, and of how good the lighting had been for the Third Degree scene in Fernandel's picture.

"I still think OUR FRIEND," Mary said, clearing her throat of the final delicious crumb and looking around stealthily, "would know just how to handle rats like those gangsters."

"He just went into the kitchens," Anne said, "so it's all right. I do too. There's something so knowing about him, really so hep. You have the feeling he has been everything, so he *knows* everything. You know what I mean. It wouldn't matter what the situation was, really . . . he'd have coped with it before. . . ."

"Speaking of the situation," Mary muttered, hunching down her shoulders and barely moving her lips, while her eyes tried to narrow themselves correctly and instead got very large and started to send off flashes of obvious excitement, "take a look. Fast."

The mother was sitting with her back to the door, and she

felt her skin prickle a little as she saw Anne's eyes focus like Mary's, and then their two faces turn clamlike and withdrawn.

She started to turn around to see what they were looking at, but Anne whispered urgently, "Not now," and she was obedient, watching the girls' eyes follow the slow passage of someone, or maybe even some*thing*, across the restaurant from the door toward the empty dim bar. They looked rather pale suddenly, as if they had eaten too much on top of watching too many reels of trumped-up tension, which was true. The mother gave herself a sharp rap on the spiritual knuckles for having permitted it, and turned around brusquely, to lend what she could of calm balance to the abrupt change in everything.

An elderly man dressed in black stood uncertainly by the large center table banked with baskets of fruit, trays of little brown pots of caramel custard, and half-empty bottles of cognac and cherry brandy and so on. His face was thin and of a peculiar leaden gray color. His eyes were invisible in the deep sockets under his shaved head, and his ears, which had very long dead-looking flabby lobes, stuck out in a manner which was for some reason sinister instead of silly. He wore a dull black scarf wrapped tightly around his throat, and there was a general air of furtive shabbiness about him.

Mary said in a light way, trying to make it sound as if she were talking of the price of pumpkins, "Wonder what's in that suitcase."

The mother said mechanically, "You should not talk about

people in public in another language," but she, too, was wondering about the small black valise which the man had put carefully between his legs and the big table. She felt foolish to find herself thinking, quite in tune with the obviously over-stimulated children, that it could easily have a time-bomb in it: ordinary people did not carry such "little black bags" around with them, and certainly did not put them down so silently in the middle of deserted cafés. . . .

"People don't usually come into places like this looking like that and carrying mysterious little black bags," Anne breathed, in a way doing it aloud for her mother. "I don't like it. He looks awful."

The oldest woman turned back to the girls in a hearty would-be healthy way. "Nonsense and fiddlededo," she said, feeling falsely like their aged aunt instead of their dam, and agreeing with them but believing it necessary to behave with reason or however it was a mother should behave in a suddenly echoing blank restaurant in a small French town when her eyes were still blinking from an afternoon spent under the torture-lights of the American Third Degree with Fernandel, and when a small sickly old man behind her made her feel frightened. Why was she frightened? What of? She was impatient with herself, and still uneasy.

"Maybe he's hungry," Mary murmured. "He's looking at the grapes. Now he's reaching down for his bag."

"Maybe he's going to snitch a few, the poor man," Anne whispered, her eyes as big and pointed as black tulips.

"Oh, rubbish," the mother said, her heart beating faster.

"He's reaching for a gun probably," Mary said. "No doubt about it."

"Oh, for Pete's sake," the mother said, but she turned around carefully, in time to see the man slide the small valise carefully along the floor about six inches, so that it rested against the leg of the big display table. He pushed one foot gently against it, and then put his right hand slowly into the pocket of his frayed overcoat, which hung sad and black down his thin legs.

"Yes," Mary remarked in a very small voice. "Reaching for his gat all right."

Then the door between the pantry and the bar banged open like a shot. The three Americans, alone in the place with the queer old man, jumped in their chairs.

Léon ran a couple of paces into the room toward the four of them, and stopped and recoiled.

"Oh," he cried out, his eyes popping at the man. "Oh, thunder of God!"

He turned and ran back into the pantry toward the kitchens.

"What a beautiful rich accent," the mother thought between two thumps of her heart. "Will I ever be able to roll it out like that? No."

A quick look at her children told her that they were in a state of frozen excitement. Their faces were pale and masked, with half-open mouths like sick fish in a neglected aquarium, and they were twiddling with their fingernails in a way which always betrayed fear or worry in them and which equally invariably annoyed her.

"Don't do that," she said, and turned back without looking again at them, toward the old stranger.

He seemed to have been upset a little by Léon's dramatic yelp, and he leaned down toward the black valise again and then straightened uncertainly and looked around him.

His eyes could not have seen the three politely gaping foreigners. His mouth in the gray face looked like a mean slit of a thing, and it was appropriate, quite part of the movie Anne and Mary had just seen, that they and their mother next watched him pull out a bent brownish cigaret and a lighter.

He sucked one interminable drag out of the cigaret, and then let smoke trickle out and up, over his cheeks and his invisible eyes in their deep skull-pits and into the quiet air.

"Why doesn't Léon come in again or somebody come in or even the phone ring?" Anne sounded a little desperate, and the mother looked sharply at her, pinched and pale, hunched over her folded arms as if her belly were suddenly hollow instead of full.

As was usually the case when anything happened which troubled or bored any of them, the woman wondered for a few long seconds if she had been wrong to bring them to a foreign land, to a place like Aix where in spite of their friendly busy lives they would always be strangers, tall and slow among the quick dark little people who had been born there for two or three thousand years. Then, also as usual, she reminded herself that anywhere at all, even where they seemed to look more like the others, in California or New York, they would be victims of the same occasional moments of trouble or boredom. . . .

"He does look rather odd. But there are Quaint Characters in San Francisco," she murmured. "I think it may be the lighting. Or maybe the way he holds his cigaret?"

Mary shifted her flashing gaze deliberately away and out toward the big fountain in the Rotonde. "I don't care for it at all," she said in a small tight voice. "Something is indefinitely not on the up and up here."

Anne looked even more pinched at this bald pronouncement and leaned miserably over her folded arms as if with pain and inner cold.

Outside, buses and trucks, and people pushing baby carriages, rolled by as always, but inside the deserted restaurant the air seemed very dead and hollow since Léon's exclamation and his sharp about-face. It would have been pleasant to hear the sound of people rattling teacups in the glass room, dice in the bar, plates in the pantry. . . .

The mother shivered, and said in a rather stupid but well-meant trial at warming things up a bit, "Now's the time when the Boss Dog should take over and save us all."

Behind her the old man coughed, in a rattling peevish way.

Anne said sharply, forgetting her polite low restaurant-voice, "Look. Quick."

39

Mary turned away from her resolute observation of the world outside, any world at all but the one inside the window, and the mother swung around in her chair again.

The shabby man had plainly put a pear from the display table into his overcoat pocket, and his left hand, thin and gray, was reaching for another, when the swinging door to the pantry crashed open and the Boss Dog came straight at him, head down and the white ear stiff with purpose.

The man grabbed for his battered little black bag, and a ripe peach fell heavily to the floor.

He straightened.

The dog gave a kind of gargling yelp, and both girls made somewhat similar animal sounds which could mean almost anything horrified or pained or astonished, and then the man was holding the dog up in the air with surprising strength, and pounding and rubbing his short white fur, and the dog was licking his face with juicy and ferocious happiness, and altogether it was a heartwarming sight indeed.

The mother and her two girls beamed and sighed, and felt almost dizzy with relief.

The man held back his face from the dog's long pink tongue, and for the first time his eyes showed, brown and bright and smiling. He pushed the Boss Dog down gently, picked up his little black bag, and together the three hurried across through the bar toward the pantry, just as Léon pushed open the door.

He stood aside, grinning, to let them pass, and then waved

his napkin apologetically as he came toward the Americans' table.

"Excuse me. Forgive me," he said. "I was looking for Madame's dog. That gentleman is Madame's uncle, the richest as well as the best nougat-maker in Provence. Our dog spent his childhood and part of his youth in the family candy factory. They are very good friends, as you can see. He still goes back to the old place for his vacations . . . watches the sugar-bins and so on. . . ."

Léon delicately picked up the squashed peach from under the big center table, and folded it with correct waiterish discretion into his napkin.

"Our dog prefers pistachio nougat, which Monsieur the Uncle's factory makes better than any in France and therefore the world. But Madame tries to limit him. Very rich. Bad for the liver. Bad for *his* liver, that is, and VERY bad for his figure. Especially bad for his disposition, in large amounts, naturally."

He sighed, and from their table removed the plate with the tag end of ham rind on it.

"That suitcase," he said. "Monsieur the Uncle won't carry the new ones Madame gives him, and he wickedly brings it stuffed with pistachio nougat, *always*. By day after tomorrow life won't be worth living around here. Snap, snarl, growl. A liver crisis."

Mary looked after Léon as he went to put the plate just inside the bar door where the calico cat who attended to mice could take a sniff at it before the evening trade started, and then to leave the squashed peach for a minion to send one further step along the line toward disintegration. (He would probably eat it. . . .)

"This proves something," Mary said.

"It proves," Anne said in a prim way, "that even heroes can be human now and then. Well, not human exactly, but less noble than heroic."

"Human will do," the mother said.

"Anyway," Mary said, "I think we ought to make a point of coming back after school for a little snack, day after tomorrow." She looked speculative and already a little amused. "I'd like to see the Boss Dog with a bad liver."

"Yes, let's. It would be mean, but let's," Anne said. "I'm starved."

"You can't be," the mother said flatly but without any conviction. "Anyway, that's day after tomorrow."

"You might stop on the way home for something, maybe some of the famous Provençal nougat," Anne said. "Pistachio nougat, of course," and she giggled happily.

"Don't. I'm thinking of my figure," Mary said, trying to pull in her stomach.

As they opened the door, Léon ran toward them, flustered at not having helped them with their coats, school books, purses, packages, gloves, and a small length of dingy knitting Mary was carrying around with her in case she felt like sweating through a few more stitches.

"Pardon, pardon," he begged breathlessly. "Always such

excitement when Monsieur the Uncle drops by. He sent Anne and Mary each a bar of pistachio nougat. He noticed the two nice little girls as soon as he came in."

The two nice little girls looked at their mother, and all three of them felt abashed and embarrassed, remembering how they had stared at the shabby sinister old man, and how they had felt hostile and suspicious.

Even Anne was not hungry for a few minutes.

But by the time they had crossed a few busy six-o'clock streets and waved into a couple of small shops they liked especially, to a cabinetmaker and a saddlemaker who seemed to enjoy waving back every few days, they felt all right again, and Anne peeled off enough of the beautiful silver paper around her bar of nougat to take a long and enjoyable sniff.

"Pooh to my figure," Mary said, having watched her closely.

"Pooh to day after tomorrow?" the mother asked.

But it was too late.

The Time He
Made the Front Page

Aix is one of the rare towns that improve. The more you know it, the better and finer and rarer and more satisfying it grows, like a few people, wines, cheeses, and books.

By the time Anne and Mary had got their teeth into the French language, at least in the present tense, which was sooner than they had expected because at school they either had to sound like the other pupils or wilt with silent loneliness and hunger, they knew several wonderful places in Aix besides the Cours Mirabeau. Of course everything seemed in an almost mystical way to stem from the Cours, or lead to the Cours, or run alongside the Cours, but it was fun to get off it occasionally, if only for the purpose of getting back to it.

By the end of November, when dry leaves rattled in the

gutters and mittens began to be useful as well as decorative, the two little American girls had decided on their favorite shortcut in all of Aix, which is full of them.

It was called the Passage Agard, and one of the two main reasons they liked it was that it was a twisting narrow alley, partly covered over by buildings and at one end not even wide enough for the two of them to walk abreast, with all transportation forbidden except *feet*, so that they could dawdle heedlessly in the front of the little shops full of perfumes and shoes and typewriters and not get knocked down by bikes or Vespas or normal-sized cars.

The other main reason was that they often met the Boss Dog there.

He evidently felt some of their predilection for the Passage Agard. It stemmed from the Cours Mirabeau, of course, just above the Deux Garçons, through an innocent-looking doorway known to very few people with less than a month or even longer to spend in Aix. It looked as if it would lead up some stairs to an apartment with children in it and a cook boiling potatoes for lunch. Instead it plunged in a rather dank way right through the old buildings, and then widened a little for the small shops on either side to catch a bit of light, and then it dawdled past some stores full of beautiful old clocks and teapots and suchlike, under a high arch on the top of which was a music school which sent out rich tootlings from trumpets and tenors, past a rather bloody little meat shop and a wonderful window full of parrots-mice-squirrels-crickets-in-cages and now and then a baby fox or a shivering monkey, and it came out triumphantly, with a real feeling of achievement and accomplishment, right by the Palace of Justice and the Prison behind, and the big oblong square.

The Boss Dog always headed directly toward the law courts and the jail. He plainly had important leads there, to what was inevitably, given the locale, the underworld of Aix.

Anne and Mary saw him oftener as the days grew colder, on their noon trot from Sainte Catherine to the little café of Madame Paoli on the marketplace across from the Palace, and then home through the Passage Agard. He seemed to be watching and waiting, in his own nonchalant fashion. He looked as debonair as always, and his recognition was curt, if not actually stealthy.

"He leaves a little trolley-cart here, a little trolley-cart there," Mary said to her mother over her pre-lunch tomato juice in the sunny glassed terrace of the third-rate warm welcoming shoddy café Madame Paoli seemed to run solely for them and the market-people.

The mother had easily adopted the habit of waiting there at noon for her girls. She would sit in the window and watch all the children chugging home for lunch in their little berets and dark blue clothes, and when her own two gangly kids came coltlike past the big Roman fountain she would feel gay, and give a nod into the bar to the sleepy waiter, and he would produce the usual glasses, stepping warily over Lucifer the black tomcat and an assortment of poodles, spaniels, and dogs: Madame Paoli, a short square woman with a big bite out of one of her ears, loved dogs, and mostly her fecund Fatima, a quasi-pseudo terrier, or perhaps a Boston or Brook-line. . . .

Today the mother asked, "Trolley-carts? I think you mean calling-cards."

"Yes, Mary. For heaven's sake. *Mon Dieu*," Anne said.

"Don't mix French and English," the mother said mechanically, it being the hundredth or perhaps thousandth time. "And anyway, I honestly don't think you girls ought to say *Mon Dieu*."

"All the kids say it at school. Even Mère Tassie says it. It is not taking the name of our Lord God in vain at all, if that's what you mean," Anne said. "In French, that is."

Mary added, "If you smile when you say it, or raise your eyes over the horizon," and then before her mother could question her possible sarcasm or even agnosticism, she went on, "I always say trolley-cart because I like it, but I know you say calling-card. Anyway, we know what we mean. I may be just a little more delicate. Dogs leave those little signals to pass the news along."

"Sometimes fourteen or fifteen without a single drink of water. It's amazing," Anne said. "I know I couldn't manage that. One wonders . . . one asks oneself, to translate roughly."

"What news do you suppose the Boss Dog has sniffed lately?" The mother looked at her watch: it was about time to move on for lunch.

Anne and Mary debated this in detail on the way home, and the general agreement as they pounded single file through the Passage Agard, crossed the Cours, and rounded the corner by the fountain with dolphins flipping and spitting merrily, was that with all the strange characters and even lawyers coming in and out of the Prison behind the Palace of Justice, the Boss was plainly on the path of some activity on the local criminal levels.

"He can't resist it," Anne said. "It's in his blood. I know exactly how he feels."

"My God," the mother said. "I mean, *Mon Dieu*. Wotcha hear lately from de mob?"

"No, seriously," Anne said as they sat down at the table five minutes later. "You can tell by looking at the Boss Dog that he knows the Underworld from long ago, even from *birth*."

"Seamy side of life. Always shows its seams, I mean," Mary said. "These potatoes with olives, green pepper, garlic, anchovies, tomatoes, and all that and so on, are a masterpiece."

"I'm starved," Anne said with Phoenix astonishment, ever new.

It did indeed seem, toward the end of November, that the cocky haughty dog from the other end of town was spending a lot of time up in the district around the Prison. The three Americans often saw him from across the square as they met before lunch at Madame Paoli's, and they found themselves comparing notes over their little bottles of thick tomato juice or tinny-tasting grapefruit.

The Boss had passed them heading north, his white ear on high and looking full of the devil; the Boss had skulked swiftly past them, nose to ground and black velvet ear dragging, toward the back of the Prison; he had pretended to snap at a fly on the edge of the marketplace but had obviously been stalling for time to get into the Palace itself. . . .

Pasteurized calories and bottled vitamins mounted to their heads as the kind tired waiter plied them with One More Drink, and they talked gravely, in the slanting wintery sunlight: Gyp, the Terror of the Terriers, was in town, while his master, Clancy-the-Con, took the hot baths at the Hotel Sextius for his aching back . . . Ming Too, the loveliest little blonde Pekinese ever owned by a gangster's girl-friend, was in town with a maid while her mistress waited in Paris for Clancy-the-Con to feel better . . . meanwhile three mongrel toughs from the caravan of a temporarily incarcerated gypsy were haunting the left wall of the Prison for a signal from their Master in Cell 11. . . .

It was all mild and pleasant, and as always it was fun to watch the rhythm of the long market-square between the little café and the Palace.

Three times a week that square was filled, crowded, teeming with hundreds of people and with orderly rows of stands, sturdy tables set up each time anew by the people who sell food and flowers and such. They had their regular places, marked discreetly on the marble-granite-cement-asphalt pavings, and you soon got to know where the man with vanilla beans would be, or the old woman with little sacks of wild lavender, or the people with finest apples, tomatoes, onions, potatoes, bananas, beans, everything.

There were trailers which almost magically lifted up one side to become tidy toylike meat markets. There was a glass-walled truck filled with red and wine-red and pale-red carnations. There was a man who squeezed fresh coconut batter from North Africa onto metal sheets and baked it into macaroons before your eyes. There was even a man, now and then, who wandered happily in and out singing patriotic songs in several languages, including his own private one . . . he did it for smiles or pennies, pushing a matronly old sheep dog in a baby buggy, she wearing a beat-up straw hat with always a fresh flower stuck in the band. . . .

The market-square is bean-shaped and like a few other things in Aix-en-Provence, such as the five-sided circle of *La Grande Fontaine*, otherwise called *La Rotonde*, with the biggest fountain splitting-splashing-spluttering, it is peculiar in its un-squareness. It also has three names.

At the top, where Anne and Mary used to come from school, it passes the somewhat chilly old church dedicated to Mary Magdalene, and it is called *Place de la Madeleine* for that.

Then there is one of the almost uncountable fountains of Aix, the town of many waters, and perhaps because of the tall Roman pillar in the middle of the fountain it is not called the Roman fountain officially, although most people do who live there from birth: it is called Preachers' Square around it! Certainly there is no obvious connection. . . .

Further down, where the twisting hooded exciting Passage Agard leads off secretly onto the Cours Mirabeau, it is called the *Place du Palais de Justice*, which is more logical because the Palace is right there too. And all the time it is one long slightly sloping market-square, three days a week at least, with shade trees and benches for the old women with baby carriages and their knitting and talk, and a newspaper stand, an ice cream stand, and not only the Roman fountain to cool the air in summer but a few monuments.

One of them, when Anne and Mary were there, had several plump undressed goddesses lolling on it, which little imps of the town always managed to keep nicely pink-cheeked, red-lipped, feverishly nippled and so on; the American children disapproved of this pipsqueak vandalism in principle, but could not help laughing whenever the makeup had slyly been refreshed.

And in front of the Palace itself are two noble and fairly honorable statues of famous lawmakers of Aix, bleached by the sun of Provence and some centuries of bird-droppings. One has lost his nose, during a revolution. The other, questionably pleasanter to look at, sits to the right of the Palace steps with a haughty vigilant air, and there at his feet, on November 29 of the year the Yankees were witnesses, sat the Boss Dog, at about twelve minutes past noon.

Anne and Mary and their mother were tippling as usual in Madame Paoli's little café across the square. "I'm tired. I'm indefinitely exhausted," Mary said dully, sinking away from the pallid glass of tinned grapefruit juice in front of her.

"Sit up and have a drink. Please, I mean. You'll feel better," her mother said unfeelingly.

Anne sipped delicately at her Perrier water, which was what she always ordered since she had read an advertisement saying that it not only helped cure gout, liver fatigue, diabetes, and milk-leg in nursing mothers, but added sparkle to the complexion.

"The trouble with Mary," she said, licking some bubbles off her upper lip, "is that she got ink all over everything again today. These juicy French inkwells are just too tempting and splashy."

"Oh, you," Mary said. "Form of tattle-telling. I'm disgusted."

"Look," the mother said. "I've been working all morning and I came up here to have a little drink with you ladies and if you can't pull yourselves together you can jolly well. . . ."

"There he is," Mary said, sitting up and taking a big swig of her fruit juice. "Excuse me for interrupting. Hah! Something's up, eh?" Her eyes were snapping with curiosity.

Yes, the Boss Dog was sitting tensely under the statue to the right of the Palace steps, the statue with the nose. He looked surprisingly like it, except for the robe and the book of law and perhaps the fat behind and the tail: haughty, vigilant, every hair of him on the ready.

"*Merde, alors,*" Anne said quietly, having sensed instantly the drama across the square, the tenseness. "What do you think . . . a murder, maybe?"

It was a non-market day, but there seemed to be an unusual amount of bustle under the statue, in the place where the macaroon man usually set up his little bakery truck, unless he bowed out seasonally to the tall fat man who made mayonnaise in twenty-two seconds with a beater which cost practically nothing. Men were unloading what looked like theatrical flats, and a few people late to lunch were standing in the cold air watching and talking, leaning on their bicycles.

Anne and Mary and their mother paid for their drinks and crossed to the little crowd: Madame Paoli was having corsets fitted in Marseille, and the waiter did not have any hints to offer about what was going on.

"Well, it's simply the season," a man in a big raincape explained kindly to them. "The *santon* stand is going up. It always goes up now, four weeks before Christmas. Naturally. You'll see." He seemed to feel this took care of everything, and jumped on his bike and went flapping off fast toward his veal-cutlet-and-salad.

"It must be official," Mary said. "Anybody who can put up a stand in this market and leave it for practically a month is *something*, a king or very important, that's all."

Above them as they stood watching, the Boss Dog observed them coolly. Anne looked up at him. He dropped his soft velvety ear a little lower toward her, and then turned away with a half-stifled yawn and what she dearly hoped was a wink.

"What's he got on his mind?" Mary asked softly.

"Something sinister."

"Oh, pooh," the mother said. "What's sinister about *santons*? They sell them every year here in this little stand. I remember hearing about it, but I didn't realize it was time already. People put them in their family *crêche* . . . like our Mexican *Natividad* but in Provence. What could be sinister about Christmas and little painted clay figures? You embroi-

54

der the truth about that dog, let's face it. Let's take another look tomorrow. I'm cold. Let's go home. I'm hungry."

"No," Anne said gently. "I'm the one who's hungry in this family. Remember?"

"Me, too, if I may presume," Mary said. "But Anne's right. That dog senses that something is up."

"It's not up yet," their mother said. "But they're putting it up. It will be up tomorrow."

"Haha terrible," both girls said in a friendly way, and they went single-file-Indian-style through the Passage Agard toward home. As they disappeared into it they took a last look back, and the tired waiter flapped his apron twice at them, once for Madame Paoli in Marseille, but they were looking at the Boss Dog, noble and remote at the statue's marble feet. And that afternoon he was invisible at the Glacier.

The stand was indeed up the next morning, and open for business.

It was simple: a homemade trailer with the wheels off and one side that flapped down to show shelves and shelves of the little and big clay figures, very bright in fresh paint, that were as necessary to Christmas as anything but breath itself: the Holy Family, the Three Wise Men, the patient donkey and the mild-faced cow, and then everyone who could possibly be found if the Baby Jesus were to be born again in any village of Provence: the Mayor in a tall silk hat with his official belt across his fat stomach; the snoozing young shepherd and the amazed one with his hands raised as if frozen toward the Star, his wife frozen thus beside him; the pretty girl from Arles in her tiny bonnet of white lace and black velvet; the sturdy miller with his floury clothes. . . .

It was easy to talk with the family who made all the magical funny solemn little figures, and Anne and Mary came soon to stop there, even in the noon rush.

And at night after school, which gets out late in France, the warm light from the little stand looked cheerful and welcoming to them as they crossed the long black tilted square toward home. They stopped often, and before they knew it were saving their snack-money each day to buy a tiny *santon* instead, the size about an inch tall instead of the bigger ones or the even tinier one called "flea," but each with its own face, kind or cranky according to the part he played in the story of Christ's birth in Provence.

There were goats and dogs and even ducks in the right sizes, too, no bigger than half-peas, and Mary spent one miserable hour, halfway through December, trying to find a beautifully painted guinea hen about the size of a grape seed which had slipped through a hole in her school pinafore. . . .

The people who spent their lives making and painting the little Christmas images were named Fouques, and were quietly renowned in all that part of the country. They looked alike: short, with large dark eyes and beautiful hands. They set up their stand every year for the month before Christmas, each time with some new models, which the husband had designed, and the wife had then helped him cast and bake and paint, and people both rich and poor came to add a new shepherd, or a village scold, or a baker or a hen, to the family Nativity which everybody arranged during that month in that part of France.

As Anne and Mary were to see, in churches and meat shops and drugstores, there were perhaps millions of *santons* in Provence, waiting in boxes and bureau drawers, in cupboards, attics, and other quiet places, for the yearly rite.

If by some miracle they could hear the call of a tiny trumpet, like the one the angel Gabriel is supposed to blow for humans on the Judgment Day, the whole country would seethe and rise like boiling milk with their awakening: small as the smallest green peas at the end of the pod, or tall as men or clothing-dummies; painted in crude clay or arrayed in real satin and real linen; any way or size they would make a mighty band indeed, and Mr. Fouques's gay reverent additions over many years would swell the ranks with honor.

By Christmas they were all out, lovingly placed around the countless mangers in corners of the humblest farm rooms, the fanciest restaurants. There might be a candle burning, or the latest invention in indirect lighting or neon. Sometimes the Baby Jesus did not appear until midnight of Christmas Eve, when he first did. Sometimes the *santons*, except for Mary and Joseph and the Donkey and the Cow, were placed far across the room from the holy stable, and each day they were moved a little nearer, all to be there on the Night.

In the churches, people reverently brought little pots of

herbs and winter flowers, or a few eggs in a greasy basket, or even a bunch of the last grapes or the three best potatoes of the crop. . . .

Anne and Mary and their mother, that month before Christmas in Aix, absorbed the gradually rising excitement of the *santon*-stand as if they were blotters, which in a way they were, for all the sounds and smells and pushings around the bright island where Madame Fouques stood smiling behind the counter in her Provençal clothes, and her husband the *santonnier* waited discreetly down on the pavement to help people choose what they wanted without breaking or perhaps snitching anything.

Only four nights before Christmas Eve Mary was relieved to witness that a young French sailor who had been prowling unhappily around the stall was finally able to buy the six or seven basic figures in the one-inch size, having received his pay, to send to his baby son in Brittany. Madame Fouques wrapped them before his (and Mary's) eyes and marked the package Air Mail and would not let him pay the postage.

The American mother, only slightly discouraged to find that the smallest figures rightly and logically cost more than the big ones, bought a whole *crêche* in what was called flea-size, about the height of a woman's thumbnail. It was in a vague way Chinese to her and in an equally vague way that was what she wanted. She felt fine about it.

Anne bought Mr. Fouques's fanciest Baby Jesus, of pink painted wax and blond hair made of nylon, all lying strangely but reassuringly upon a woven bed of wild thyme and sage and lavender picked in the craggy meadows of Provence. It smelled good.

The three foreigners made a little *crèche*, which they would have called a *Natividad* at home in California, on the seventeenth-century gray marble mantelpiece in their enormous drafty room, which smelled of drains until then. They put the whole thing together at once, instead of doing it more correctly day by day until all the figures could kneel or stand amazed near the Nativity, because the mother had decided to flee the friendly and yet closed doors of Aix for the even older city of Marseille, where she and her girls would be so completely foreign on Christmas Eve that they would be too busy to feel lost from their own land and all the cousins and suchlike holiday bustle. . . .

The night before they left, with school closed for ten days and Mr. Fouques's *santons* keeping their hearth warm for them, spiritually at least, they ate supper at the Glacier, to warm their own hearts and stomachs.

By now they knew where all the madly wheeling buses and electric trolley cars stopped and then went to, and in an hour or so they would dash for one marked "Marseille" and hop in.

By now they knew when the Grand Fountain would blaze with light and when it would have to be silent and hideous for a cleaning and general mop-up, not spouting nor spitting nor splashing nor even spluttering.

By now they knew that Léon, the waiter, loved them in somewhat the same fashion and with the same intensity that they loved him, and Angelo only slightly less so.

That night everything conspired toward perfection, as it should just before Christmas if not always: their bags were properly in the bus check-stand; the fountain was at its most spectacular blazing best, floodlighted to the nines to celebrate or at least announce Christ's birth; it was not Léon's night off, and the way he flicked his napkin at them was a kind of embrace, very gay and good. They felt at home, which is a fine way to feel in any country or language.

Mary, with a nod from her mother the banker, decided to follow the first and higher-priced of the two menus, with enough minor changes to prove that she was still an individual and not a gastronomical slave-type. She substituted raw sliced Alpine ham for whatever it was the chef had said would come first, and herb omelet for the grilled trout that was supposed to come next, a large green salad for the chicken or steak of the next course, and a strawberry ice for the dessert. She eliminated the cheese and the fruit. In other words, she ate a fairly light and simple meal, but with the reassurance that she was actually ordering the heavy indigestible rich expensive one marked on the menu.

Léon noted all her requests seriously, with only one subtle and, in fact, practically nonexistent wink to the mother-banker-dietician of the family, to let her know he would supervise the correct charges at the end of the meal. By now he was in cahoots with all three of them together as well as each one of them separately.

Anne was tired. The past days had been almost too full for her, feverish with having to wash white gloves and pack and

60

say Merry Christmas to right and left. The thought of eating was too earthly, too exhausting . . . she murmured of a small cup of consommé. "Or perhaps just a wing, maybe even a small-small tiny leg of chicken?" Léon's voice was almost not there, like the devil's. "With a touch, a taste really, of Sauce Suprême? And just a spoonful of rice?"

Anne heard that satanic murmur. She agreed wanly.

"Then perhaps, perhaps," the voice went on softly, "one leaf from Mlle. Mary's green salad? After . . . well, after, there are apricot tarts as I remember. But since *la petite* wants strawberry ice instead, maybe I could bring the apricot tart, too, and leave it on the table, in case *she* changes her mind. . . ."

The pattern was familiar: after half a cup of strong broth Anne snapped to attention like a revived rubber plant, graciously accepted half of Mary's thinly sliced ham, polished off a large portion of rice and chicken swimming in a heady sauce, and made it both possible and necessary for the quiescent placid delighted mother to order some more green salad. It was necessary to order more tarts too.

Part way through the second one, Anne put down her fork with a look of startled questioning which for a moment resembled the indigestion anyone could have expected in her. She hurriedly half-gargled half-spat some sounds.

Mary put down her spoon. "Try again," she said gently, managing to imply that her sister was sometimes uncouth. "Try some of this *sorbet*. Delicious. Non-fattening."

"Try breathing deeply, or take a sip of wine," the mother said.

"Oh, rubbish, and *thank you*, Mary," Anne said with comparative clarity. "All I mean is, where is he?"

"Who? Where is whom or do I mean who? Don't wave your fork around like that," the mother said. "Who is *he*?"

"Murder," Anne said.

"She means, where is the Boss Dog," Mary said. "Ain't that right, pal? Or as you often say you were taught at school," she continued, looking tauntingly at her mother over a large spoonful of pink ice, "*où est la plume de la queue de la chienne de ma tante sous la table*?" And she went off into a high cackle of enjoyment of her own kind of wit, which is of course one of the pleasantest of all such personal delights.

Anne looked coldly at her. "I am perfectly well able to explain myself," she said, dangling a syrupy baked apricot on her fork.

"Don't wave it around like that. And I hope I don't have to ask you again, because if I do I'll get unpleasant," her mother said.

"Oh-forgive-me-I'm-so-sorry-it's-the-last-time," Anne said. "Mary is right. Where is he? Here we've been all evening, and no Boss."

"He's probably out on the tiles," Mary said, and went off into another high cracked cackle.

Her mother looked expertly at her flushed cheeks and then at the restaurant clock, and felt thankful that the bus would be along in twenty-three minutes: she had at least one emotional drunk on her hands.

"Dogs don't go out on the tiles. That's cats," she said.

"It does seem strange to me," Anne murmured, deftly and discreetly removing a cookie called a *gaufrette* from Mary's plate. "Will you please ask Léon? He can't spend *all* the time up there on the Place?"

"*I'll* do it," Mary said giddily. "No need to bother our old gray *mère*. And my accent's very good tonight. And you may have that *gaufrette* if you want it."

The reply they got was disturbing: Léon shrugged, raised his eyebrows, pulled down his mouth, and in other ways confirmed his statement that the Boss Dog was neglecting his usual chores there at the Glacier.

"He's here one minute and gone the next," Léon said. "It may be the holiday mood?"

"How does he seem? Worried? Depressed? Nervous?" Anne asked, quietly wringing her hands over her polished plate.

"Gone. Mainly plain gone," Léon said, shrugging again. "He is preoccupied, undoubtedly."

"Love?" Mary asked, stifling an enormous yawn with no luck.

Léon looked at the mother, stifling what might have been an equally enormous grin. "No," he said seriously, "I think it is more like business. Some financial arrangement perhaps. Perhaps a legal settlement of some kind. . . ."

"It's true he's been up around the Palace of Justice a lot lately," Anne said, and then the Marseille bus swung around the fountain, and they all dashed and scrambled and ran out in a shower, a hail, a veritable storm of Happy Christmases.

Which it was: everything was fine and merry and windy, and when they got back to Aix it was so good to be in their high beautiful room with the gay little *santons* on the marble mantelpiece that it was almost New Year's Day before they did much but stretch and snooze and put away things people had sent them from California.

The first day out in the clear washed air of the town, with the giant plantain trees black and bare but not at all sad along the Cours Mirabeau, they went up through the Passage Agard to the bean-shaped square in front of the Palace.

It was not a market day. It was not even a school day. Mr. Fouques's little shabby wagon-stand was gone. Somebody had put another touch of lipstick and judiciously placed rouge on the big naked females at the end of the square, and it was possibly the same imp who had made the nosed one of the two famous judges look very red-nosed indeed in the winter cold.

Anne and Mary and their mother waved to the nice waiter in Madame Paoli's little café, who flapped his napkin wistfully through the glass porch at them, and then they walked at a healthy trot down the Cours to the Glacier: they knew it would be almost too voluptuously warm and steamy, with surely a big tureen of soup for them. . . .

Toward the end of the meal, which naturally expanded itself far past the Spartan limits of the soup bowls, Anne asked her mother, "Put in a word about him, eh?" and Mary said, "There is fresh pineapple today. Where do you suppose he is? Make a few inquiries, eh?" and the mother said, "Léon, we've been wondering about. . . ."

64

Before she could finish, Léon said in a quietly furious voice, which any good waiter can employ at will, "Ah, that fellow! That bounder! He became so insufferably conceited that we could stand it no longer!"

The children stared at him, sunk back in their chairs.

He slapped nervously at some crumbs, and moved the water carafe three millimeters north-northwest.

"Why?" Anne asked finally, in a small voice.

"Well, it was like this. We could in the end stand no more of his posings and all his affected barkings for the movie-cameras . . . *sound* cameras," Léon went on, almost strangled with exasperation. "We simply gave up, and sent him down to the nougat factory. Let him get a bellyache there. Let him have one of his migraine headaches even! He was becoming insufferable with conceit."

Anne and Mary looked quietly at their friend. Their forks were idle.

He suddenly realized his unprofessional excitement and glanced nervously around: his stylish employer was bent over her cash books at the desk, and the three Englishmen, two Dutch ladies, and three Danish exchange-students were noses to plates. He bent toward the children and their mother.

"You are apparently not up to the minute," he muttered. "You apparently and even conceivably do not know of what that dog did."

They shook their heads, with a kind of shame. They felt stupid.

Léon leaned over them, informing them of important things they had neglected to observe. . . .

"On Christmas Eve, the Eve itself," he said, in a kind of stuttering rumble which was very impressive, "on this past Christmas Eve, while you were wherever you were, enjoying yourselves I hope, and all of us were here serving a large somewhat gay crowd, that dog singlehandedly stopped a major robbery, and who knows but what he may also have prevented something like a murder, an active killing!"

He stood back, and unprofessionally touched his napkin to his brow, which was dewy.

Anne and Mary stared up at him, their faces pale and their mouths open with shock, delight, and astonishment at the romance of the moment.

The mother stared, too, with only half one spiritual eye still left on the wind-twisted waters of the Grand Fountain, the black naked bending branches of the trees outside. Léon tasted his moment as only a good waiter and/or actor can, and leaned near them again.

"You know Mr. and Mrs. Fouques, the famous *santonniers* of the Palace of Justice steps?" he asked almost in a whisper.

"Certainly," Anne hissed back at him, hypnotized.

"Boy, oh boy, do we know the Fouqueses!" Mary murmured, but even she did not pay much attention to herself, for Léon was saying fast, in case anybody should come in for a new table or call for a bill, "That night, that sainted night of the Nativity when good people except for waiters are mostly in their own warm homes, a gang of outsiders, evidently with well-laid plans, moved in from the alleys around the Palace and behind it! It is said that they even came at a signal from the Passage Agard! They converged upon the innocent *santon*-stand, at a moment when almost everybody had gone home and the exhausted Fouqueses were about to close shop for another eleven months. . . ."

Mary said, "And of course there was a lot of money there."

"It was absolutely rolling in, pouring in, when we left. . . ." Anne moaned.

"You are right, you are completely right," Léon cried, delighted to have such agile stooges. "Money! That was the lure! This band of clever ruffians was about to seize every penny our famous *santonnier* had earned in months and months of infinite creative toil. . . ."

"Creative, yes," the mother murmured, her mouth slightly open like her children's, and her mind's eye seeing the tiny resolute figures on the mantelpiece around the pink wax Baby Jesus.

"The work of an artist," Léon agreed with her. "And our dog, who had been, as far as is known, keeping an eye on the gang for some days, gave such a ferocious savage alarm that police and civilians came running from every direction. Even poor underpaid lawyers working hard into the night for their clients in the Palace of Justice threw open their windows and applauded."

Here Léon gave an ironic and theatrical cough, to keep up his reputation as one of the town's loudest dissenters. He permitted himself this delightful indiscretion only with such friends as he knew as well as the back of his own hand, and the girl's mother felt flattered.

"I'll bet the Boss Dog was sitting under the Judge's statue," Mary muttered, her eyes withdrawn, dwelling on the scene.

"Right, right," Léon said. "He hurled himself down into the mob. . . ."

Anne shuddered with vicarious excitement.

Mary looked as if she were searching for something wise or caustic or merely intelligent to say. "Then what?" she asked finally, for Léon was waiting.

He smiled. "Hah! Our dog continues to bark madly, snarl, growl, yap. The Fouqueses realize the plot and the danger. They too agitate. People come on the run. The villains are caught with their filthy hands in the cash-box. Mrs. Fouques gets her little Provençal cap knocked off. A few *santons* are broken, but they are only the cheap ones and in the main all is saved. . . ."

"Thanks to, . . ." Mary interrupted in spite of herself.

"Thanks to We Know Who," Anne finished for her, cheeks flushing with happiness and pride as she reached for a piece of bread Léon had forgotten to take off the table.

"Oh, how awful that we missed it," the mother said. "It's really wonderful."

"Yes, We Know Who," Mary said a little crossly to Anne. "But what I want to know is, where is he?"

Léon flipped the mustard and salt off their table to the next one, and a few crumbs onto the floor. His story was plainly almost over. "As I said," he continued in a low voice, "our dog became insupportable, absolutely. Such conceit. Papers from Marseille and even Avignon sent photographers, and he posed so much his neck got stiff."

Mary let out a crow of amusement. Anne laughed too.

"It made it very difficult," Léon said. "He was always posing for curious customers, right in my path."

He dashed away, and brought back the check later in a satisfied way which means, with a good waiter, "No more time for chit-chat but I love you," or something like that.

"No wonder they had to send the Boss off," Mary said as they got into their coats, scarves, mittens, and so on for the cold blowy walk home. "I'd need more than pistachio nougat, though, if I had to rescue the Fouqueses' *santon* money, and then be photographed and all that."

"Not me," Anne sighed. " 'Not me' is perfectly correct in French. In fact it's the only way you can say it."

"All right, all right," said her mother, who was thinking how good bed would feel in the big graceful slightly smelly room that Madame de Sevigné was supposed to have slept in. "Not me. If our room's good enough for Madame de Sevigné, it's good enough for me, even with the original mattresses."

"Too much *vin rosé*," Mary said.

"Who, me?"

"Yes. It makes you think about bed. But I still say I don't blame the Boss Dog for letting his neck get stiff. All that publicity and all those crowds and photographers. . . ."

Anne sighed loudly over the stiff wind. "That's my idea of heaven," she said. "And I wouldn't care how stiff my neck got."

"You couldn't give any autographs, though," Mary said around the front of her well-wrapped mother. "If you were a dog, I mean."

Anne peered around, too, coldly. Then she looked straight ahead, full of disdain, and asked, "Is there any little sort of snack or banana or cookie or anything at all to EAT, at home?"

"Not everybody can be a star," Mary said.

"What?"

"I said that I'd like to have four legs, like the Boss. Get home faster. Get our old lady into bed." And Mary let her warm mittened fingers give a reassuring squeeze to her mother's, and trotted a little faster.

"That Boss Dog," Anne said, half envious still, and then they all held hands fast and ran down past the fountain of the four dolphins.

The Time He
Managed Everything

In Aix-en-Provence when the three Americans were there the
new year had hardly begun when the Cours Mirabeau began
to take on a strange excited look and feeling.

Slowly electricians strung colored lights across it and
along it, a great extravagance. Piles of gaudy signs were gradually distributed and then hung over it: laughing plyboard
clowns and animals in high silk hats and pretty girls in spangles. Side streets were hung and bedecked almost as wildly, if
they were on the route for the three Grand Parades or would
have rows of shooting galleries and sideshows on them.

Finally, about the first of February, the technicians started
trying out all the festoons of lights for the great Carnival,
which would last for about twelve days before Lent began, and

for several nights the electric current dimmed, and whole districts of the old town blew their collective fuses, in order to have everything blazing and perfect for the fiesta.

Anne and Mary had three little friends who lived high above Aix in the dry piney hills where old Cézanne used to have his studio, and the five of them had noticed, walking from school for tea parties and suchlike, and well before Christmas, that in the carefully closed warehouses called the Covered Market, on the way up, great things were going on.

They soon nosed out a couple of passably wide cracks to peer through, and thus managed to keep an eye, like countless other children of the town, on the gradual building and painting of all the gigantic images for the Parades.

There were the floats themselves, to be fitted whole or in pieces over big trucks or horse-drawn carts: things like a kind of cricket fifty feet long, with eyes that would be moved by the men hidden inside them, and long delicate trembling feelers covered with sparkling diamonds, and then maybe fifty laughing baby-cricket-heads made of molded *papier-mâché* which fifty little costumed children would wear to prance along beside the huge mother-bug.

There was a whole story on a float, for instance: a huge miller, maybe thirty feet high and with a very fat belly which would move in and out with two men inside pushing it, to make it look as if he were snoring, and then in the piles of enormous flour sacks he lay on, dozens of mice as big as puppies, running on hidden tracks in and out of the holes in the sacks.

For this float there were fantastic mouse-heads for more dancing prancing children alongside on the street, and Anne and Mary peeked enviously at them. They longed to be chosen to ride-run-dance-stagger-even-*crawl* in the Carnival Parades.

One of Anne's school friends was going to ride in a huge gold and satin music box, with some other girls and boys dressed in the white powdered wigs and the brocades of the royal court of Marie-Antoinette, and it was tacitly agreed between the two little Americans and their mother that *if* Anne were a French girl and a citizen of Aix-en-Provence, there could not possibly be a more perfect choice for the Queen herself than Sister Anne. As it was, the agreement was equally tacit that it would be indiscreet to expect to be anything more than visitors, which is what they all were, even though they had stayed somewhat longer than most of the people who had been flocking to the fountainy city for 2500 years or so.

They bought Carnival programs, and resigned themselves to spectator roles, along with most of the other citizens and visitors. There were to be the three usual Parades, on the first and second Sundays and then two days later on Mardi Gras as Lent was to begin. In between, a hundred more or less exciting events were to roll off, like a bicycle race at the football stadium, and the annual Children's Ball at the Municipal Theater, when all the seats would be covered by a floor of planks and the costumed children would go crazy while their dazed proud parents watched from the dingy gold and velvet boxes above them. . . .

Anne and Mary decided to go to the First Parade on the Cours Mirabeau simply to see what it would be like from the sidewalk, with tickets for the grandstand down at *La Grande Fontaine* for the second Sunday and, of course, for the Ball on the Thursday afternoon between.

Their mother lined up all the tickets, and they bought black velvet masks, Anne's with a kind of flap of black lace, partly for glamor but also very practical against mouthfuls of confetti during the high excitement. They had all agreed that their costumes would stop with the masks, since as visitors they ought not to risk winning the first prizes, the only ones they even considered.

The opening Sunday was cold as Billy-be-damned, and except for the giddy lights-banners-shop-windows-and-people, very bleak indeed. This was according to schedule: in fact some of the habitually glum Carnival-hounds insisted that it would snow at least once during the twelve days, most probably on Mardi Gras itself when the *papier-mâché* King would be crowned and then burned in a gigantic bonfire by *La Grande Fontaine*, and it was rumored that the pharmacies were putting in extra supplies of cold remedies, and that the local hospitals were readying the pneumonia wards.

Anne and Mary and their mother put on everything warm they owned, including two pairs of mittens for Anne, navy blue over red over bluish red hands, and about eleven-thirty, when they thought everybody would be in church, they went up to the top of the Cours Mirabeau near the statue of the King René, where to their slighted affronted astonishment they found that fences had been firmly closed all along the route; that Boy Scouts with blue knees, red noses, and gay neckerchiefs stood ready to protect the gates with their lives; and that everybody else in Aix had decided to skip the eleven o'clock Mass and make it up sometime during Lent.

The crowd was so surprising to the three Americans that they crept by several back streets toward Madame Paoli's peaceful little café across from the Palace of Justice. Everybody else seemed to be with friends. People shouted and slapped shoulders and kissed babies, and the foreigners suddenly felt very much so, very timid and strange. And Aix suddenly felt almost hostile to them, with the cold wind blowing and the distant taunting sound of a band or two. . . .

"I think a drink is in order," the mother said, playing her trump card doggedly, the one she counted on most faithfully when the jig seemed up.

"Glug," Anne said, looking pinched and sallow.

"I couldn't eat a thing," Mary said, over the whoops of seven little boys dressed as Red Skins who pelted past her in the opposite direction, toward fun and life and rowdydowdy companionship and everything she did not have, gone forever maybe in the bitter February air.

"I didn't say anything about eating," her mother said, to keep up a semblance of frozen vivacity, "but I think perhaps a cup of hot bouillon *is* indicated," and she went on walking as fast as she could to the café. The truth was that she felt somewhat weepy: the children on the sidewalks seemed so very gay, except for her two. . . . She touched the black velvet

75

masks in her topcoat pocket. "Hey," she said, "you should put these on, so you can be invisible."

And they did, although the chance of hiding their long solid bodies in the swarms of the small gadfly children of Provence was faint indeed. Anne and Mary laughed suddenly at one another, Anne with the black lace flapping and the mask-eyes cut glamorously long and slanted, Mary looking rather like Herbert Hoover during his most cherubic period. The mother felt better.

The staid *Place du Palais* was mad, openly and ungrudgingly mad.

Children dressed as everything from King Kong to two-legged mermaids climbed over the solemn juridical statues, fell into the fountain with the Roman pilaster, slipped on the pigeon-dung in front of the church of Mary Magdalene, jumped with shouts from the austere window ledges of the Palace itself.

Several brass bands from neighboring towns stood in straggling knots, tootling and banging in chilly but hilarious anticipation of the long march through the town.

Parents clutching little powdered countesses and big-headed mice and crickets, and, of course, cowboys and Donald Ducks and pirates and so on, pushed and yipped through the thick crowds.

Above everything loomed the floats, which during the night had been pulled, bumping and tottering, through the quiet streets from the Covered Market. Grotesque, brilliant

76

in their new paint, they nodded and leered above the puny humans. . . .

It was infinitely more exciting than Market Day, impossible though that would have seemed until now.

Anne and Mary pulled their mother in a kind of warm daze to their little café. They had forgotten the cold wind and the fleeting gray climate of their souls, and already the drunken joy of Carnival was invading them.

Inside Madame Paoli's, it was bedlam.

She rushed toward them with a shriek of uncalculated friendship: they were, she was in the habit by now of assuring her faithful customers, *her* foreigners. And the children liked her because she was so honest about it and about that one ear which apparently had a big bite or slice or chunk taken out of it, which she did not attempt to hide under her hair. The mother also liked her for various kinds of honesty and because she made *couscous* every Thursday, being a French-Algerian, and a *couscous* as good as hers was hard if not almost impossible to find.

"Quick quick QUICK," Madame Paoli shrieked that morning, jumping down from her high cash desk and flapping a path through the crowd around the bar with her best blue silk apron. Her face was red with excitement and the pressure of her new corsets, and her half-ear peeked proudly from her freshly crimped hair. "Sit down at this table by the big window in the corner! I insist. You can see everything, absolutely everything this way! You can stay here all day. Ringside seats, eh?" She looked triumphant, and shoved people brutally aside, to make way, and the mother followed her to the front corner table in the glassed porch, trying not to cringe with embarrassment at having this kept for them, all unannounced and unplanned and unreserved. Nobody seemed to mind: the tables were gay with fresh cloths over their usual cold marble tops, and the thick goblets sparkled, and through the glass wall the bands sounded almost majestic as they stamped feet and tooted on the Palace steps.

"Isn't this divine?" Anne said. "Ringside seats indeed." She was in the Royal Box at the Opera. She sat regally straight, beautiful behind her black lace mask. . . .

"No Lucifer-cat today," Mary said. "No visiting poodles and collies to see Fatima or whatever that sexy café dog calls herself. I bet lunch will be absolutely delicious, with flowers on the tables and everything."

Gradually every seat was filled with townsfolk and villagers bound and bent on fun, and the wintery light looked warm through the bottles and glasses of pink wine from the nearby hills, and the old waiter and his two harried relief-workers darted like gadflies with plates of a special meal in honor of the whole wingding of Carnival. Everything took twice as long as usual and cost twice as much, and was worth it, in a completely forgettable way, because of all that was going on outside the thin glass wall.

More and more children fluttered and simpered by with their parents, to assemble before the official start of the Parade behind the Palace. Anne at times felt almost sickened, to

78

see their silly little faces behind the makeup and to think she, too, but for a slight accident of birth and nationality, might be thus rosy-lipped and thus silkily garbed. She was forced, in spite of the succession of odorous courses of super-extra dishes set before her which she rapidly polished off, to sink back now and then, pale with envy.

"Hah!" she would say with quiet ferocity. "There goes Mireille Tondu! Just look at her. That little stinker. She probably thinks she looks beautiful, in that pink satin thing."

"She's crazy if she does," Mary would agree loyally, a grilled mushroom stuffed with chicken-liver dangling from her fork and her wide eyes following a schoolfriend who minced happily by, dressed as a lady-in-waiting, or even a mouse or a cricket.

"Mireille will be unbearable at school tomorrow," Anne said, plunging bravely into the next course.

"School in general will be unbearable," Mary said. "Too much noise. This town goes too crazy. I wish we were in the middle of San Francisco Bay in a little rowboat. In a heavy fog. This town takes too long to work up to something. I wish we were in that fog." Suddenly the mother wished they were too. The prospect of eleven more days of the mounting din and excitement almost frightened her. She took a reassuring or at least bracing sip of the *vin rosé*.

Halfway through the meal, the several municipal and military bands visiting from other less carnivalesque towns began to shape into lines instead of clusters around the Palace steps, and their leaders, all portly and hung with gold braid, eased their post-dinner belts for the ardors ahead. Their noises took on a definitely promising rhythm.

Children yelled shrilly around their assigned floats, and fell down under the weight of the headdresses and got picked up like chessmen, and a few got stomachaches and either marched on or threw up discreetly and were taken home.

Boy Scouts blew whistles everywhere, like hysterical birds. The wind blew, too, but everybody seemed to be laughing and singing so much that it was unfelt, unheard, and inside the draughty glass porch of Madame Paoli's little café the happy human beings warmed the air until Mary shed about three layers of blue wools, in which she had been eating until then like a kind of gastronomical cocoon.

The First Parade was of course slower than planned in getting under way, and the three Americans sat until late afternoon in the pleasant friendly room.

The surging, fairly orderly boom and bang outside, with the swaying tottering monstrous figures prancing around all the great ponderous floats, melted into a digestive dream for them, not nightmarish at all but certainly not real. Now and then they saw Bernadette Bulidasse perched on top of a ten-foot carrot, or were sure they recognized Jean Andreau's snub-toed shoes under the big white disk of a cardboard pocket-watch trudging alongside a giant clock filled with pretty girls proving that "It Is Later Than You Think" or something equally silly. . . .

And the bands played loud and crazy, and faster and faster the thousands of normally staid citizens grew loud and crazy too. Instead of kissing their cousins and slapping shoulders with their second cousins, they began to kiss strangers and slap shoulders with people who might be the lawyer or the undertaker or even an avowed enemy, and behind their masks their eyes were bright and blank.

At the end of the Passage Agard, when Anne and Mary and their mother finally and reluctantly left the comparative tranquillity of Madame Paoli's café, two Scouts and a smilingly intent man in a liver-colored suit collected money from them and gave them tickets which allowed them to walk but not sit down, and they went onto the Cours Mirabeau, which was lined with firm fences made of old grape-stakes and which behind the fences was crowded with a mob of almost hysterical people. The Parade was passing, under the four rows of giant plantain trees.

Thanks to the several hours spent in their ringside seats, and to the months of squinting through cracks in the Covered Market walls, the girls knew every float, and good digestion made it possible for Anne to see Mireille high in her satin powder-box with only a shudder instead of a thorough attack of jealous vertigo.

"Oh," she moaned, "that little brat! She's plainly freezing. Can't take it. No sense of *theater*."

"They all look tired to death," the mother said. "I'm glad you're down here with the mob. They have another hour to go."

"At least," Mary said. "Let's go sit down. I can't see anything, because if you may remember, I am not even nine years old and am not quite as tall as some other people I could mention."

Her voice trembled, even above all the noise, and one quick look assured her mother that she was dog-tired. Her cheeks were too bright, her eyes were too large and luminous, and in general she gave all the signals of having heard, walked, eaten, seen, and smelled beyond her absorption-point.

"Let's have a drink, eh?" The mother pulled out her trump card for the second time that day.

"Oh," Anne moaned again, above the crowd-roar. "There goes that little old Bernadette. Smirk smirk. I bet she thinks she looks just darling. Hah."

"Come along," the mother said, going into reverse as best she could in the thick bold shrieking crowd along the fences. "There's the Deux Garçons. Hold on to me."

At the usually meticulous and persnickety old café the tables were sticky with spilled fruit juices and the sidewalk underneath was littered with cigaret stubs and the first coating of confetti. On either side of the patch of crowded tables on the sidewalk, men sold paper bags of the stuff, blue, green, pink, and people were beginning rather cautiously to throw a little here and there.

A table was miraculously free as the three headed for it, and they sat down and ordered two lemonades and one large brandy. The mother gave the girls money for confetti. The noise was astonishing and almost numbing, and it did not occur to them that it would soon grow ten or eighty times louder.

An old man was selling packets of wild lavender against one of the big trees, and on the other tree by the café terrace another man with a big pot on three legs stirred hot sugared nuts in a kind of molasses. The cold air was turgid with all the smells and food and people.

"What was that picture-taking Madame Paoli was talking about?" Anne shouted, toying with her straw the way she had seen French pictures of American teenagers do, and looking wistfully at a band of about a dozen masked girls dressed in pretty Provençal skirts and bonnets, shrieking along the street tweaking at men's arms-coats-trousers.

"Oh, yes," Mary said. "Something about Fatima. Group picture with her children. She wants us to be there."

"Who? Us? Is it dogs or people?" The mother was yelling, but nobody answered, for suddenly all the lights went on, brilliant as flowers, and people stopped and gaped with pleasure, so that a kind of gasp went up, as if the town itself had caught its breath, and then everybody began to shriek again under the bands and ribbons and ornate shells and rococo clusters of colored bulbs overhead, along and across the stately old street, turned drunken for twelve days.

"What?" the mother yelled, and both girls leaned toward her patiently and mouthed, "Picture. Madame Paoli. She wants us to be sure to see the picture being taken."

"What picture?"

"That's what we asked you," they said.

They were all of them tired, the mother said, so she managed to change her sharp response into a somewhat doggedly companionable smile, and after catching the half-mad waiter and paying, they started down the Cours.

Perhaps twenty steps along, there was a frightening yell-roar-sob from the milling people, and they seemed almost to be sucked out into the street through the open gates: the Parade was finally over, the bars were down, and it was time for the official Confetti Fight.

Everyone ran, jumped, screamed, pushed, and threw the little spangles of soft-colored paper as if hurling handgrenades, into the air, into people's faces, over hats and hair and down open bodices, from edge to edge of the wide black street. On the sidewalks, too, the ones who had been comparatively staid and quiet began to act as if they had breathed a magic laughing gas. Men linked arms, stranger with stranger, and ran shoulders-down against groups of shrill half-crazy giggling girls. Confetti was everywhere, on the people and the tree trunks, and already inches deep in the cracks and gutters. Vendors hawked it everywhere, and baldly charged double and treble for it as the piles grew higher and the sound-pitch with them.

Anne and Mary quivered like frail craft in a storm, and felt bolder as their own hair and eyes and coats changed colors; their fistfuls of the stuff went out with more bravado.

One nice old lady walked primly along, without a single drop of paper on her, and Mary went up and very respectfully sprinkled a handful across her shoulders.

"Mary!" her mother called, trying to be stern. But it was impossible: the old lady had disappeared forever, inwardly if not otherwise unsullied, and the two girls were wildly pelting their soft dry warm paper-snow at everybody in their paths.

High up in the bare trees, loudspeakers blared helplessly from the broadcasting station by *La Grande Fontaine*: a lost baby was waiting for his mama at such and such a café, a parked car would be hauled off in ten minutes if not moved, Georges Brassens would strum his guitar on Disque Numero 00000. . . .

Underneath the trees sixteen thousand people howled and ran zigzag and bumped together and then ran zigzag off again, and there was no sound of their footsteps because the confetti lay so thick on the pavements.

"It's crazy! It's crazy!" the mother cried to a friend wearing a false nose.

"It's Carnival!" the friend yelled back, managing to look like a famous professor, which he was, and throwing a fat handful of pink confetti smack in her face.

The children's mother spat and spluttered, and said helplessly, "Why, Raoul, you. . . ." But it was too late: the friend was gone, into the mob of other professors, thugs, senators, and suchlike, hiding behind their false noses.

Anne was within reach, holding her black lace flap fastidiously over her mouth with one hand and aiming a blob of confetti at a good-looking cowboy with the other. Her mother grabbed at her, feeling suddenly that she had listened and submitted to enough.

Mary was gone.

"Oh, she's around," Anne yelled, letting out a satisfied

shriek of false protest as the cowboy stuffed some confetti down the neck of her coat.

"No," the mother cried. "She's not. When did you see her?"

Anne could not remember, and the next few minutes were ugly ones in a restrained way, as they went back through the wild pushing crowd to the Deux Garçons and then back again. At about 50 Cours Mirabeau, halfway to the Big Fountain, where doctor-friends had a high apartment where they went sometimes to look down on the serene old street, the mother looked up: Mary might have taken refuge there.

"Look up! Look up to the balcony," she yelled to Anne, trying not to feel trembly.

"Yes, look up, look up," a tall man mimicked her in bad English, and threw a handful of confetti straight into her open mouth. She choked and spat helplessly.

"That's mean," Anne cried in French.

"Mary," the mother yelled, and this time the man threw confetti hard against her upturned eyes. She bent down, blinded for a minute.

"Well, it's Carnival," the man said, perhaps a little abashed by Anne's angry eyes glaring at him through her velvet and lace mask.

"Dirty idiot," she said clearly, with an impeccable French accent picked up during recess on the schoolgrounds.

He went off, alone.

"People by themselves at carnivals," Anne said, taking her

mother's arm, "are even worse than the ones in gangs. Or so I now feel. Are you all right, you poor old thing?"

The mother had to go and lean against a building, because of the way her eyes hurt. She knew they would wash themselves clean, and as they did so she saw that the mean lonely man had mixed cigaret tobacco with his confetti, somewhat as in other and perhaps more brutal days people would put pepper or acids into theirs, in Venice. . . . Mary was not anywhere.

They got off the Cours and headed along the quickest route for home, but she was not there. It was dark and all the street lights were on, and the roar from the Cours sounded like animals in an enormous circus.

They crossed the Cours again and went up the streets toward the Covered Market, and then realizing how futile it was they turned back to the Deux Garçons where there was a public telephone.

The mother tried to be reassuring, and indeed it was true that Mary was perhaps the most practical, solid, and resourceful human being in her experience. Even so, Anne, knowing it, too, seemed to shrink and turn wan, like a little candle flickering in too cruel a draft.

There was a table at the back of the café, by the toilet and kitchen doors. They ordered a hot chocolate and a brandy, and Anne sat mutely while her mother telephoned the two people in Aix she knew with telephones too. There was no answer at either place. She assured herself that she felt odd because telephoning always made her feel odd, but she hated to go out of the stinking little booth to see Anne again.

In the impossibly crowded noisy smoky café, where confetti lay on the tables and even on the ancestral rubber plants in the center of the beautiful old room, Anne was bending tensely over the Boss Dog.

Someone had stuck a red paper rose through his collar, and his fur was bespangled with pink and green and yellow dots. In a totally unprecedented way his black left ear lay trustingly, intimately, on Anne's knee under the table. His tongue was far out.

"He needs a drink. Badly. Did you find her?" Anne asked.

"No, but I'm sure it's all right," the mother said, feeling worse and worse, with one eye still weeping from the tainted confetti and the other too bright. "He'll have to wait for a drink. Please go home, Boss."

Anne stood up, straightening his rose and then her mask, and he slid off through the legs of everybody.

"Let's go," the mother said. "I'll tell the waiters to watch for her. They all know her. We'll go back along the Cours and then home. She's probably just flirting with a handsome Davy Crockett or something."

"Hah hah," Anne said. "Not that girl. She's probably rescued an old lady, or a lost baby, and is at the police station waiting to be awarded a Fulbright Fellowship."

"Congressional Medal, not Fulbright. I mean Carnegie," her mother said. They hurried out. The Cours was worse than ever, but they kept their heads down and their mouths shut, and held hands, and made fairly good time.

"The Boss Dog looked quite natty," the mother shouted, mainly to drown out the sound of her sickly beating heart. She had reached the stage of blaming herself not only for letting Mary drop her hand, but for ever getting on the trains-buses-planes-ships that had brought them here.

"He came right in and saluted me," Anne shouted back above the mounting wildness of the street. "He looked absolutely bushed. OW!" she yelled in her most American accent, as another handsome cowboy slapped a handful of confetti hopefully at her collar-line. She turned like a bee in flight, and yelled back, "*Salaud!*"

"Don't say that," her mother yelled just as loudly. "It sounds awful."

"This is Carnival," Anne cried mockingly, and then held her mother's hand more tightly. "Mary will be at the police station or the first aid station. You know, behind the Fountain, right across from the Glacier. . . ."

She stopped so abruptly that her mother almost fell against three very old men in black corduroy suits covered with confetti who came unsteadily toward her.

"Ah, the lovely big lady, the pretty girl," one of them sang, and she thought it was nice of him, because at that moment she felt like neither lady nor girl, but as old as the hills.

They swerved by.

"Don't do that, Anne," she snapped. "It almost killed us."

It is a feat to snap loudly in an enormous crowd of hysterical people, but she did so, and then felt ashamed of herself.

"Don't pause in mid-flight like that," she said more reasonably. "You almost tore my arm loose."

"Mary is indefinitely at the Glacier," Anne said, peering through her battered but still glamorous mask. "I know it. I feel it. Useless to go to the Police. The Boss Dog told me."

"Oh, hell. I mean nonsense."

"No, honestly. He came right up to me and for the first time in his life, I mean my life, he put his hand, I mean his paw, on my knee. You saw. It's obvious. Hurry, is what I say!"

She almost left the ground, so sure was she. Her soggy cold heavy little feet were like blackbirds skimming over the confetti. Her hand was like a warm mitten full of vibrant bird bones, pulling the mother passionately down the Cours, through the crazy yelling feckless people.

"You'll see," she cried out once.

They stopped to pant and puff, leaning against a drugstore which had been carefully boarded against the crowds.

"That dog is magic," she cried. "A magician. A wizard. You'll see."

The mother understood how much Anne was trying to comfort her, and she said to herself that it would take only a minute more, and in such a case another minute cannot much matter, to stop at the Glacier before they went around and past the great silly splashing fountain to the Police and the first aid station. Her heart still thudded with near-panic, but Anne's hand in hers felt good.

The Glacier was even worse than the Deux Garçons, being nearer the bus terminals and the station and the big reviewing stands where the judges and famous visitors had sat shivering and beating their hands together.

There seemed to be twice as many tables under the bright lights in the glassy rooms and on the wide sidewalks, and extra waiters held their trays high as they skimmed here and there with drinks and sandwiches and silver cups of lemon ice.

Anne and her mother looked in for a minute from the littered street. The cold wind blew up confetti in little curls and clouds.

"It's too late. It must have taken us a half hour to get here from the top of the Cours," the mother said. "Let's go straight around to the Police."

"No. We go in here," Anne said, sounding much older, at least forty-five, and without another word they did go in, and walked past the center table covered with oranges and apples and one pineapple and the usual lot of hopefully tempting bottles, and into the room behind. Nobody paid any attention, for the people sitting at the jammed tables were tired and cold and thirsty and full of Carnival, and buses were leaving every minute or so. . . .

"We should say something to Léon, if we can catch him," the mother said, feeling bewildered and desolate. "It may be his day off."

"Hah," Anne said firmly. "He told me he makes enough tips during Carnival for a two-week fishing trip. Hey, there he is!"

91

"Léon, Léon!" the mother called out blindly.

"No, not Léon, Dopey. Excuse me. Not Léon. It's the Boss Dog, going into the back room. He got here."

She dashed across the big room, past the crowd of customers at the usually empty tables by the bar, and through a frosted glass door marked *Vestiaire*, where cartons of vegetables and canned goods were piled against one wall, and where in the cold months the waiters hung their favorite clients' coats on three ancient wooden edifices called hat trees.

The mother followed numbly behind her little girl. She felt in a kind of fever of fright for Mary, the solid true-blue-tried-and-true one, the practical and unfrightened one. An eye still wept, protesting its blow of nicotine, and her heart felt as if it were being squeezed of its own bloody tears.

The unused cloakroom was dark and warm. Light from the kitchens seeped through a dim window in the wall above the cases of food, and against the opposite wall, on a pile of neatly folded winter overcoats, Mary slept like a babe.

Beside her the Boss Dog sat in his most wearied way, with his big Buddhalike bottom spread all about him but his head still erect, the black ear sweetly lolling down, and the red paper rose perky in his collar.

The mother permitted herself the indulgence of letting her other eye flood and spill over, once and once only.

"See what I mean?" Anne whispered, clutching at her.

"How did he get here, is what I'd like to know," the mother murmured. "There he was at the other end of the Cours. . . ."

"He knows all the secret ways. Obviously. He got here just as we did. Anyway, he has four legs. Let's wake her up."

Anne went over to the Boss Dog, and said in her purest richest most rolling and most gurgling French, "Thou art the loveliest handsomest most intelligent and most delicious dog in Aix, in Provence, in France, and without contradiction in the world." •

He looked up at her in the dim little room, with all the blowsy noise outside, and gave a kind of puff, which for him was quite undignified or at least unbuttoned, of obvious satisfaction.

Then he slowly stood up, and walked past the two women and pushed open the kitchen door, which closed behind him.

"He knew where Mary was and then he found us and then he came back," Anne said softly. "He's a miracle, that's all."

Mary was as refreshed as a buttercup after rain. She awoke at the sound of their familiar voices, and said, "Oh, hello. I'm sorry I left. I couldn't find you, so I was sure you would know I was here, because the Boss Dog saw me." She yawned, rolled onto her feet, and started to hang up the unknown overcoats.

The mother felt like saying a few tart things, the usual reaction in parents to such a situation, but she did not because aside from them she felt so happy. She hung up some coats too.

Outside, Léon came skimming frantically toward them through the jam-packed café, with a tray on one hand loaded with empty glasses and bottles, and a fistful of large bills in the other.

"Ah," he said. "She was here all the time, eh? You found her, eh? She's a very intelligent girl, eh?"

He whipped past them through the kitchen door.

"I think maybe a drink is indicated," the mother said in a vague pleasant way.

"Let's go home," Mary said. "I'm quite tired of all this noise, indirectly."

"We could cut through some back streets. I'm tired too," Anne said. "I've been under quite a strain." She blew some confetti off the front of her coat.

"Léon told me there are some belly dancers in the first street off the Avenue Victor Hugo by our dentist's," Mary said. "He said they weren't worth looking at, except maybe for their bellies."

Léon whipped toward them again with two trays of clean glasses.

"Thank you," the mother said. "I was worried."

"It's nothing nothing nothing," Léon said sideways over his shoulder. "I just piled up the coats. The dog brought her in, and I knew you'd be along soon. She sleeps easily, eh?" And off he skimmed.

Mary buttoned herself dreamily into her top layer of blue wool, yawning and fumbling. "That was comfortable," she said.

The mother managed to keep her mouth shut, although she felt a little peevish after the pain of worry and doubt.

Anne tapped her foot. She had pushed her black lacy mask

up on the top of her head, where it looked delightful, and her mother thought it was just as well there were no mirrors nearby for Anne to catch herself in, or they would *never* get home.

"I think the Boss Dog looks absolutely terrible," Anne said as they got off the Cours. "He is doing too much. He has circles under his eyes. Even his white ear looks droopy. He is leading too many lives."

"Too much noise is what it is," Mary said. "It got me, and it's got him. He needs to get away from this Carnival-deal, that's all."

"Back to the nougat-mines," Anne said.

Suddenly the mother felt fine: she would give the tickets for a box at the Children's Ball on Thursday to a friend with nine moppets; she would take a bus to Marseille and then Hyères with Anne and Mary; they would get on a boat for the Golden Isles. . . . They would flee Aix-en-Carnival, as they had done Aix-en-Noël!

She looked around happily to see if the Boss Dog was with them. He should come along too. But of course that was impossible, and of course he was already off somewhere, either back watching the prisons behind the Palace of Justice and across from Madame Paoli's, or out in the kitchens of the Glacier seeing that the *bourride* had the correct amount of thyme in it. . . .

They trotted past the fountain with four dolphins.

"Good thing I met him," Mary said suddenly.

"Good thing he met *me*," Anne corrected her.

The mother agreed.

"I'll be glad to get home. I've got confetti in my panties," Anne said impressively.

"Impossible," the mother said, but it turned out to be true.

The Time He Appeared Indirectly, If at All

By the first of May the tender leaves of the four rows of giant plantains along the Cours Mirabeau in Aix have formed a ceiling above the wide black shiny street, and by the middle of the month they have grown so thick that it is like a long high cave . . . or as it had first seemed to Anne and Mary and their mother, the year before, they were indeed fishes at the bottom of a mysterious green river. They swam up and down it dreamily, especially Anne, who felt that she understood fish better than anybody.

"What exactly gives you that idea?" Mary asked one green

breezy day as they all strolled or drifted or swam toward the upper end of the Cours.

"I just have it, that's all," Anne said.

"I suppose you think you were once a mermaid and nobody else ever was?"

"I don't think, I know. I can still remember certain very very indefinitely clear things about many things that you do not even suspect, about being something you obviously never were."

"How about stopping for a drink?" their mother broke in firmly. "I think one is indicated."

They sat down at a little table on the wide sidewalk in silent dignity, and it was not until the glasses of fruit juice were half empty that she decided it was wise to pick up the chilly or vaguely hostile conversation again.

"I think Anne is right," she said. "Anyone who has any feeling at all about fish would recognize the Cours."

"May we ask for some 'keks'?" Anne's voice was gentle and forgiving, and they all knew that the subject had been closed on an amicable note, and they then went on to other things as they peeled the brown crumby paper off the little lumps of dry raisiny fruitcake which are apparently part of the international lingo in European bars and tea shops, like "Okay" and "Ow motch?" in stores.

"It's funny how some keks are better than others. You can tell how good the place is," Mary said, peeling her second one neatly. "They're all exactly the same, too, which is the queerest part. Belgium. Italy. Here. How is that?"

"It's like all the pictures of the brides and grooms," Anne said. "I've had two. May I take another?"

"Go ahead," Mary said grandly, and then added toward her mother, "I'm sure it's all right, I mean, isn't it?"

"Sure," her mother said. "I mean, certainly. Go ahead. Live it up. Eat twelve. You are eating like horses lately anyway. Bigger horses, I mean."

"Spring," Anne mumbled.

"Or like all the pictures of the First Communion," Mary said almost as thickly. "Let's go down the Cours, when we've finished our snack. . . ."

"Hah," the mother said.

". . . and look at the pictures," Mary went on more clearly, "of all of the kids making their First Communions."

"I'll probably see several of my friends," Anne said. "They have been doing it lately. I even see them on the street, so beautiful. I'd love to be able to dress all in white that way, like a bride, and have people look at me."

"Flapping along in those skirts and veils," Mary said with apparent scorn.

Anne said, "You feel that way because you are too young."

"Let me tell you," Mary said, leaning resolutely across the little table, "that plenty of French kids about nine years old make their First Communion and get photographed. Plenty. I know several French girls nine or eight. . . ."

"No, don't take another kek, Anne," their mother said hastily. "I think we had better walk off some of this excess of argumentativeness."

"Wow. Murder," Mary said reverently. "How would you do that in French?"

They mulled the question, not too successfully, as they headed down the Cours.

All the stone benches were covered with the old women knitting and jiggling baby carriages with very new babies in them, and the babies who had been in them when the three Americans first drifted up and down the street were now tumbling and staggering, some on little leashes, and most of them eminently sturdy handsome prospects. When they fell down, people picked them up and set them straight on their feet and then went on in a detached kindly way.

By the time Anne had daintily picked up a small boy and one fat smiling indeterminate, and Mary had carried one who was yelling toward the old lady who looked most interested in it, they were at the end of the Cours, ready to gape at the photographer's window.

Sure enough, thanks to the time of the year, it was filled with pictures of young children in their First Communion clothes. Some of the shots were elaborately enlarged, like those of movie stars in Hollywood windows, so that they seemed gigantically and impossibly beautiful. Some were colored, with deep blue eyes where they should be brown. All were plainly retouched according to the demands of emotional mothers and proud if financially harassed fathers.

"Hah," Anne said flatly, spotting a school pal. "Thinks she's pretty all right."

"Well, she really is," the mother said. "I like that pose somewhat better than the one with the eyes downward."

"Smirky," Mary said. "I know that little angel too. Plain smirky. Me, I like it when they look straight at you, holding the Rosary in white gloves. I hate it when they roll their eyes up."

"That's to show they're pure," Anne said firmly.

"And how does it prove that, may I ask? I can roll my eyes up and it doesn't prove anything."

"You know absolutely nothing about either purity or eyes," Anne said. "Personally I know exactly how it feels when you roll your eyes up."

"Not my eyes. Your eyes. Anyway, you know everything."

"It's spring, all right," the mother said.

"Anyway," Mary went on, with a quick look to catch her mother's expression as well as voice, and an equally quick change from bellicosity to gentle amiability, "I think it is very interesting to see how you can tell how rich the families are by the way the children are dressed in the pictures. That boy is plainly rich, because he has a white suit on, and it costs a lot to have a white suit dry-cleaned, and anyway he'll wear it once."

"And that one is poor, or at least with a more practical family, because he has on a navy-blue job which probably belongs to his cousin anyway, because it doesn't fit," Anne said, playing along discreetly with the obvious signal in their mother's face and voice.

101

"Not necessarily," Mary corrected her. "There might be somebody ill in the family and he'll have to go to a funeral before he outgrows it."

"Murder," their mother said. "Let's walk down past the Glacier to see if the Boss Dog is there, and then go home."

"He won't be," both girls said firmly.

"It's good weather . . . lots of rich cars from the Riviera, lots of people with poodles. . . ."

"No," Anne said. "We saw Léon in the Passage Agard yesterday on the way home from school. It was his day off but he couldn't go fishing because his cousin or somebody was in labor. Twins, maybe. Premature. And he told us the Boss spends most of his time up in that quarter, sniffing around the *Palais de Justice*. We think, all three of us, that it went to his head to catch those robbers at Christmas, and that he fancies himself as a private eye or something. Léon says he may be in cahoots with a couple of lower-class lawyers. Anyway, he just can't stay away."

"Scene of his former glory," the mother said. "You're probably right. I'd do it myself, I bet. Let's go through the Passage again and stop at Madame Paoli's, just for fun. That will give us a chance to walk up the Cours again. This weather is too good. You can do your Catechisms and Grammar tomorrow."

"The day is certainly too good to louse up with either of them, if I may say so," Mary agreed. "And not many more left, either."

"Don't talk that way. Let's ignore it," Anne said.

"Can't ignore a fact," Mary said. "Which this is. We have to leave."

"Yes, it's a fact," the mother said, and they walked a little heavily for a few minutes, and then fell once more into the drifting light rhythm of the Cours and forgot or at least were able to forget halfway that soon they must go from Aix.

The end of the long bean-shaped square in front of the Palace seemed very bright after the cool pale green shade of the Cours and the narrow odorous dimness of the Passage Agard. They blinked up automatically at the main statues and sure enough there was new rouge on the fat ladies lying at Mirabeau's feet, not only on their lips, and one of the judges had a pigeon on his head.

Across the square Madame Paoli's little café looked very gay and as if it were unbuttoned, with the glass sides taken down until autumn, new plants in the boxes along the terrace, and a late-May breeze lifting gently at the striped paper covers on three of the six outdoor tables.

An unusual number of people sat at the three left bare for plain drinking instead of eating, and there was a small crowd in front.

"Nothing bad, no accident," Mary said quickly. "Everybody looks gay. Probably another First Communion."

"Mary!" Anne said sternly. "Not at this hour. Not in a café."

"Pooh. It could be carrying on from earlier, from the Madeleine. You know everything, plainly."

"Would you each like another grapefruit juice?" the

103

mother asked therapeutically. They agreed with some coldness that they would. She got between them and took their hands and headed toward the apparently packed café.

"Looks interesting," Mary said casually, giving her mother's hand a squeeze to make sure her suddenly reasonable tone had been observed.

"Yes, doesn't it?" Anne said blandly, squeezing the other hand for the same reason.

And they went smiling across the square. My goodness, the mother thought helplessly. April April or May May, laugh thy girlish laughter indeed. Up and down, up and down. . . .

At least three people were taking pictures: the omnipresent photographer with the big stylish moustache from the publicity agent, his sub-junior assistant who was trying to grow a big stylish moustache, and a cousin of Madame Paoli who sometimes helped serve *couscous* on Thursdays and was handy at almost anything.

They aimed in their several fashions, the two amateurs very tensely and the professional with great casualness and one hand idly nestling on his upper lip, at the shifting and slightly frenzied group in front of the café.

The three Americans felt shy about pushing through, and going to one of the tables still set for lunch or perhaps set early for dinner. They stood to one side, watching.

It was evidently something to do with Fatima, the café dog, and a smart gray poodle who often trotted in and out, and then several other dogs.

Fatima sat placidly, her tongue out with great daintiness,

her barrellike undistinguished body at ease, and her bright eyes merry. The gray poodle, named Dok, like most poodles in France who are not named Freeskee, occasionally sat beside her and then trotted far enough away to be shrieked back into place by several of the excited people who seemed to be interested.

There were at least six dogs on leashes: a handsome low-hung basset with sad eyes and thick bent legs; a lean racy-looking collie with a beautiful long caramel-and-white coat; a springy arrogant Airedale, sniffing and snapping at flies; three or four other extremely stylish and well-bred fellows and girls, with fine paws, pelts, ears, eyes, muzzles. . . .

"I never saw so many good-looking dogs in one place," Anne sighed happily. "It must be some kind of private club, giving prizes or something. Oh, I simply must have a prize dog when we get home."

"I suppose you were one, once?" Mary asked ironically, and then shifted her tone at a warning squeeze of the hand from her mother. "Yes, that's what we need, a thoroughbred dog, isn't it? Say a Pekinese?" She knew her mother admired them perhaps the most, in the face of widespread if repressed mirth.

"Take your choice," Anne said. "There's practically every breed right there. Why on earth put poor little old Fatima, Fatty Fatima, in there with them?"

Mary said, "Hey. This is the picture Madame Paoli was talking about at Carnival. This is the one she asked us to see. And here she is." The short corseted little friend with one and a half ears had spotted her "foreigners," and was hurrying toward them, flapping a new white silk apron.

"Enter!" she cried dramatically. "Enter and watch! Come and sit down and have a drink! Just look at everybody! A great day! Move over, Jean! Give these ladies your table, eh, Count Jossy?"

With their usual feeling of helpless embarrassment, the mother and the girls pushed gently past the people and the dogs and sat down at the old Count's table and smiled and nodded at some smiling and nodding acquaintances and strangers, and ordered two soda-waters and a vermouth-gin.

By now at least eight dogs were sitting, miraculously, in a quiet row, either off their leashes or discreetly at leash-length from their tense but laughing owners.

"NOW," cried the professional photographer from behind his moustache, and the two amateurs cried behind him, "Yes, NOW, of course," and they all crouched and clicked their cameras like machine guns, furiously, before the line of dogs yawned, stretched, and walked every which way.

Only Fatima sat, round and smiling, waiting placidly for more.

Gradually the crowd melted into the café and off over the square toward cars parked by the Palace. There was a jolly roar from the long smoky inner room with the bar in it.

"I never heard so much laughing in all of Aix," Mary said, looking at her glass to see if she could handle what was left in one gulp or make it in two. "I'm too full of fruit juice. Sounds like the Carnival almost but nicer."

"I wish I really knew what it was all about," Anne sighed. "Sometimes I find it depressing to be an outsider or just young."

"It has nothing to do with that," her mother said briskly. "Don't dramatize things. We can't know everything. There goes Fatima. She gets fatter by the day."

"Like the Boss Dog," Anne said. "Léon says people at the Glacier insist on giving him nibbles, now that they eat on the terrace in this heavenly weather, and then lumps of sugar with brandy on them. He loves brandy."

"Living in a restaurant or a café is definitely a hazard," Mary said. "Calories. Let's ask Madame what it was all about."

Madame Paoli came beaming to their table, wiping her flushed face thoroughly with a corner of her new apron. "Was it not amusing, charming, wonderful?" she stated excitedly. "Photographers! It may even be in the Marseille weekly! And just in time too. That Fatima. . . ."

She decided to sit down for a small Ricard with them, and according to custom gave Anne one delightful whiff of the licorice in her milky glass. Anne sighed happily, dreaming of being eighteen or so. . . .

"And so unexpected," Madame went on after a restorative swig. "I am exhausted. But suddenly I found by chance that at least eight of Fatima's children were in the neighborhood. And I have been planning some sort of picture for months, but it is always too late and she has another family. Quickly I seized the moment, knowing her condition again. I made a few telephone calls. I summoned my friend the photographer. What a story, we agreed!" She took another good swig.

"Impossible," the mother said with somewhat more than her usual firmness. "Fatima's children? Impossible. Fatima is a . . . well, she is more or less of a. . . ."

Mary interrupted. "She's mostly or at least about half terrier, I'd say."

"That's it. That's it perfectly," Madame agreed. "*Somewhat terrier—or even spaniel.* Many people are ignorant of it. But Marie is right. Fatima is largely or at least somewhat spaniel, perhaps water-spaniel, or water-terrier, perhaps some other type, but definitely in her own class."

"More or less," the mother added with friendly irony. "In other words, somewhat."

She and Madame snickered maternally.

"But what is this about all the thoroughbreds who were here this afternoon?" the American mother asked. "You aren't going to tell me they are related?"

Madame laughed, nearer a roar than a snicker. "I assure you on my honor," she said, her little eyes sparkling, "that they are. Yes. Positively and indubitably. Fatima is a female of infinite good taste. She has had nine families now, without any direction from us because it was always too late for us, as is currently the case, to give her any advice. I mean, by the time we felt she might need some. And each time, each time on the dot, she produces one absolutely perfect specimen."

"Each time different, eh?" and the two women laughed again as if they knew a secret together, so that Anne and Mary sighed a little and looked out across the square, quiet before people started to go home from work.

Mary turned back to them. "Do you mean, Madame, that every single one of those dogs in the pictures was one of Fatima's children? Every single one?"

Madame Paoli explained in some detail that such was the case: Fatima had a large healthy family of fine pups about twice a year, and sometimes even oftener, and in each family there was one seemingly perfect breed-type, this year a dachshund, last year a toy poodle, four years ago a wonderful wolf-dog. . . .

"People for miles around know of her amazing gift," Madame said proudly. "When Fatima is about to have another family, they come back, begging to be the first to choose a puppy. And always, always they can find at least one in a litter that will fool any but the most famous dog-show judges. It will have every single qualification of a thoroughbred!"

"Gosh," the girls said in American.

"Except," the proud little woman added regretfully, "that of course it is *not* one. Fatima is a remarkable wife and mother, but. . . ."

"Not exactly racy," the girls' mother admitted. "Ho hum and ah well . . . and Madame, we must be on our way. And when do you expect the next batch?"

"Oh," Anne said with forceful astonishment. "Is that why she's so tubby, I mean plump? Gosh!"

"Of course, dope," Mary said. "I thought you knew everything about everything! One look would tell."

"Hold it," the mother said in a low way she used only occasionally.

"In about two weeks or perhaps eleven days," Madame Paoli said, tactfully averting her ear-and-a-half from the sudden tinge of discipline or at least admonishment in the gay noisy air.

"Oh, no," they cried. "Not that long. In two weeks we'll be gone!"

"Gone? You can't go. You just came," Madame said, looking sternly at them. "You are *my* foreigners."

Their springtime peevishness vanished, and they seemed to lean closer together, almost frightened at the thought that when such an important thing as Fatima's next family happened, the way things kept on happening in Aix and probably elsewhere, even California, they who by now loved and knew so much of it would be far away. It seemed cruel and wrong.

The mother took Anne's hand across the table, and put her arm across Mary's shoulder beside her, and Madame looked on with understanding and suddenly moist eyes.

"I'll let you know all about it," she promised. "No matter where you are. I promise. And now you must have a drink with me. I insist. It is my turn. We'll drink to Fatima!"

She hurried off. The wistful old waiter was busy with the thinning but still jocular crowd inside.

"Glug," Anne murmured. "This will make three bottles of grapefruit juice in one afternoon. Can I do it?"

"Either loosen your belt or go to the toilet, or both," Mary said without much expression, and then went on intensely,

"Maybe she'll send us one of the pictures, anyway. I'd like to study it. I'm interested in various types of dogs and people."

"Not as interested as I am," Anne said firmly, loosening her belt. "I know about how a dog feels."

"Well," the mother interrupted quickly, "you'll get practically every race in those pictures. Imagine that one little smug sweet bitch producing a poodle . . . a basset . . . a . . . wolf-dog, collie. . . ."

"Not a Peke," Mary said. "Not yet, I mean."

"There are very few Pekinese in southern France," Anne said. "I've noticed that especially. They are hard to find. But there was a dachshund, and what looked like a. . . ."

". . . an Airedale, very racy indeed," the mother said. "Oh, Madame! This is too nice of you!"

The children murmured and exclaimed, too, and they all drank with polite enthusiasm, and toasted Fatima's approaching motherhood, and Madame promised them an enlargement of the current family portrait as well as immediate news, and they parted rather emotionally.

"My, such nice people," Mary said, clutching her mother's hand.

"I don't know if I can stand it," Anne said, clutching the other one.

"Certainly you can," her mother said, wondering if any of them could, and all the time knowing, having lived that long, that they both could and would.

"I've always felt completely at home in this charming little old citadel," Anne went on.

"Hah," Mary said, peering around her mother, "I can remember feeling indefinitely lost, the first days or so."

"Not I," Anne insisted. "As I look back over my past, it seems to me I have always been able to find wonderful friends. In fact," she stated loudly over the sound of several Vespas and car horns, "I have a gift for it. People like Madame, and all those little stinkers at school who think they're cute and bright and everything but are really quite nice, and people like Léon at the Glacier, of course, and. . . ."

Mary suddenly began to laugh in the special way she did when she was deeply, fundamentally, and fully amused, so that people hurrying home turned to look and laugh too.

This did not bother her mother, who was always caught up in the general mirthfulness of it, but Anne was conscious of the way they were being stared at, and she asked coldly above the laughter and the general twilight noises, "What's funny, after all? Personally I feel quite mournful, to leave Léon and the Big Fountain."

"Oh, for Pete's sake," her mother said. "You're not the only Sensitive Soul in this world. What's so funny anyway, Mary?"

She felt peevish, and assured herself that it was probably Madame Paoli's second vermouth-and-gin that was letting her down. "What's so funny, little sweet-potatoes?" she asked in apology, looking down at the children hopping at her sides along the sidewalk.

Mary went on laughing her special crowing cackle for perhaps a quarter of a block, and then simmered. Finally she said,

"Madame's next family portrait isn't going to be quite so distinguished, that's all!" And off she went again.

Anne and her mother stopped her, beside the fountain with the four merry dolphins on it, and they stood in the clear golden light of the sunset in a sudden pause of noise and movement.

"I'm thirsty," Anne said. "I wish the dear old dolphins were spitting *eau potable*."

"Don't mix English and French," her mother said automatically.

"Drinking water. Excuse me."

"I thought you'd had too much to drink already."

"I have, really. Maybe I'm just starved. As a matter of fact I am. Is there time before supper for a ham sandwich?" She was only half-joking as she looked up at her mother from the wide rim of the fountain where she sat.

"Nobody seems to know what I know," Mary interrupted. "I mean, what I think I know." She seemed somewhat recovered from her recent bout, but her face still glowed with amusement, and her eyes sent off sparks saying, "Secret, secret!"

"What do you know, then?" her sister and mother asked loyally. They had a great respect for Mary's nose for news, and were in fact quite ignorant of whatever she'd discovered.

"The clue," Mary said slowly, playing her audience like two trout on a line, "has already given it away to you! As I said, distinctly and plainly, I can hardly wait to see the next picture

113

of Fatima's prize sons and daughters. Not this one, but the one taken after she has the new batch. That's the whole point. Because there's going to be quite a surprise in it!"

They looked closely at her in the deepening gold twilight. Except for her obvious delight she seemed quite normal, not feverish or demented. . . .

She went on, gazing sideways up the street toward the Cours in a nonchalant fashion, and paddling one hand in the water, "Of course, one black ear and one white ear, and one ear up and one ear down . . . that rather spoils the racy effect, eh?"

Anne let out a very undignified yip. The two children began to laugh and bounce on the fountain-rim, and people looked pleasurably at them and hurried by.

"Oh, he's a smart one," Anne gasped. "I know dogs all right. I know them thoroughly. And he's the smartest one I ever knew! Oh, murder!" And she laughed helplessly.

"Keeping an eye on the underworld," Mary added with pride and affectionate sarcasm. "Hah! And playing the hero! And all the time secretly married!"

"Oh, that rascal," the mother cried. "That sly Boss Dog . . . he's won the prize again, . . ." and even the gay sound of the four dolphins and of all the other fountains splashing under the silken whisperings of the millions of plantain leaves in the golden air of Aix could not drown and cover the laughter of the three travelers who had stayed as long as they could. . . .

Afterword

I know at least a couple of tricks which some people consider shoddy, especially newspaper people. One is to use an alphabet, say Artichoke to Zucchini, or Aardvark to Zebra, or even Anarchist to Zoologist. I myself have been guilty of using this trick more than once and have even called on Xanthippe, supposedly Socrates' shrewish woman, although how I dragged her in for the letter x I cannot now remember. (x is an alphabetical no-no.)

Another very shoddy gambit, which is looked down upon as cheap indeed, is the tried-and-true Five ws. They are seldom even spoken about in decent newspaper offices, although their ghosts linger over or near every reporter's word processor or even the old-fashioned typewriter. Of course, the order of Who, What, Where, When, and occasionally Why varies according to current policies as well as politics, but it is useful always, and even a one-inch squib on the bottom of the last column on page six will usually comply with the old forbidden and unmentionable usage.

Myself, I am quite unembarrassed about the Five ws, and do not care who may choose to cast the first stone when I say blandly that in the year 1953 (or perhaps a year later) my two girls and I went from St. Helena, California, to Aix-en-Provence in France. We were students there, all three of us, although they were about eight and eleven, and I was past forty. Our reason for being there was simple enough: I had promised my husband not to settle myself or anyone near and dear to me until we had lived there for at least a year and then gone away for another to see if it was true that I/we wanted to return for the rest of life. Anne and Mary and I had spent more than a year in St. Helena, near Napa in northern California, and although I knew from the beginning that we would not be there every day of every year from then on, I did believe that the schools were good and that it would be a fine old town for me to stay in after they had grown away from both it and me.

Furthermore, I wanted them to learn French while they were young, almost as much as I wanted and needed to speak it again myself. (And I think that by now in this little résumé almost anyone could identify the Five ws, although as usual they could all be enlarged upon at will.)

For instance, Anne and Mary were really delightful people to be with, which I'd always known but was to prove many more times. I myself was free and happy as I grew used to the passage of time, and being again in France was part of the good-dream side of my life. As for Aix itself, we went down there because a mentorlike friend suggested that it might do for a couple of weeks before we carried out my first plan to live in Arles for a year or so. He said, in his usual mild didactic way, that although Aix was a stuffy Royalist little burg, the "mistral" did blow too much for comfort in Arles, and, of course, our two weeks there turned into a good five years in all. Although the first time around we managed to get back to St. Helena again in somewhat more than a single year.

Once home, I found to my astonishment and horror that the beautiful schools had been deserted almost wholesale by every good teacher, so that my two children simply snoozed away the next year or two as far as I myself could see. In France, they had been almost monstrously energetic and creative and excited, but in California they would sag home from school too early, by midafternoon instead of six o'clock as in Aix, and because they were not allowed by the worried PTA people to cross streets or go into parks or indeed even to breathe without my more-or-less parental guidance and protection, they seemed to spend most of their hours at home lying listlessly on their beds reading poor comics instead of savoring every weekly issue of *Tin-tin* and *Spirou*. In other words, it was a crying shame, and we returned to Aix within a couple more years, and they came to life again with a resounding and very rewarding jolt. No more gym, no more cafeteria food, and no more easy school hours! Instead, they got up and were back at school by seven-thirty every morning, and then we had two hours at lunch together on the Cours, and they next saw me

117

at suppertime. And they were back again as full members of things like Music in the Schools and the Ciné Club and even the Comédie de Provence, and so on and so on. In other words, Aix was where we *were*.

And best of all, perhaps, Boss Dog was still around town. That part was almost too good to be true for all three of us and for three very definite if differing reasons. Of course, I would never dare to ask either Anne or Mary *Why*. They were so happy when they saw him saunter elegantly across from the Palace of Justice and pretend *not* to see us sitting on Madame Paoli's pathetic little *terrasse*. My own memories, though, I think are clear enough in this little story of what we did about Boss Dog the first time around, and of what he did too. I never even wondered about his own Five ws, actively at least.

I think I wrote a few things about our somewhat peculiar acquaintanceship during the long snooze we all went into when we left him and Aix, the first time. But how can I be sure? Certainly, he was worth more than any old journalistic trick, and he knew the Five ws, backwards and forwards, better than any of us did.

M. F. K. Fisher
Glen Ellen, California

118